Lulled

… to quiet, silence, pacify, settle down, or hush

Travis N. Jensen

CYFworld
Press

CYFworld Press books may be ordered through booksellers or by visiting:

CYFworld

https://CYFworld.com

and

CYFworld Press

https://cyfworld.com/cyfworld-press-1

CYFworld Press
ISBN: 0999681389
ISBN-13: 978-0999681381

Library of Congress Control Number: 2017918412

CYFworld Press, Peoria, AZ

To all who have felt discouraged, frustrated, hurt and even lost. For those who have a desire to do more, be more and to create a lasting change towards the unity and connection we all have.

"And others will he pacify, and lull them away into carnal security that they will say: All is well in Zion; yea, Zion prospereth, all is well—and thus the devil cheateth their souls, and leadeth them away carefully down to hell" --Book of Mormon, 2 Nephi 28

Chapter 1

Mark Walker's head throbbed, his body ached and he had the distinct taste of blood in his mouth. A drizzle of blood, mixed with his saliva, leaked out over the corner of his lips and onto the cool concrete floor of his cell. His vision was still tunneled, but the light in the center of his sight slowly expanded and became clearer as he transitioned from his previous unconscious state. Mark couldn't help but think that just weeks earlier, his greatest worry was the next day's curriculum for the Sociology course he taught at the University.

Even after he fully came to, he continued to lie on the hard grey floor, not moving, fearing that movement would bring the beatings once more. He wasn't sure if any of his bones were broken. He wouldn't know until he tried to move. After a few minutes laying there in his conscious state, Mark slowly started to prop himself up with his arms. As he did so, the three who had beaten him jeered, laughed, and mocked him in both English and Spanish. Pain shot through his wrists, arms and ribs. As he propped himself up, his head pounded even more. Mark closed his eyes, winced, and then wiped the blood from the side of his mouth onto his sleeve.

An officer from the jail approached the cell. He ordered the others in the cell with Mark to face the back wall and to assume the position with their feet spread and hands against the back wall. When they did, he and another officer entered and proceeded to pick Mark the rest of the way up off the floor. They were bringing him in for another round of questioning. This already long day of interrogation was just going to get longer. He knew that this time would be worse. At the same time, he knew that too much was at stake. He had already endangered two of his students, and the cause they were engaged in was too important. Death was a real possibility, but he had no choice but to face it. He wasn't going to reveal anything. He just hoped that the others would be able to complete what they had started.

Chapter 2

3-1/2 years earlier

Mark Walker looked at the number that appeared on his pager. He dialed the all too familiar hospital line on his cell phone. When the operator answered, he asked for Labor and Delivery. A young mother had just delivered her first child, a stillborn baby girl, at Saint John's Hospital in Denver, Colorado. "I can be there in 10 minutes," he told Mindy, who was one of the nurses on service. Mark was a social worker who dealt specifically with the Labor and Delivery departments for three hospitals in the downtown Denver area.

Twelve minutes later, Mindy greeted Mark as he walked into the department. "She's in room 4B," Mindy said as she nodded in the direction of the room down the hall. Margaret Smith and her husband Jeffrey had just finished spending a few minutes with the lifeless body of their baby girl. They were both sitting on a blue-green polyester covered couch. Margaret was still crying with her head buried deep into her husband's chest. Jeffrey had a stunned and pale look on his face as he held Margaret in his arms. "I am sorry about your loss Mr. and Mrs. Smith." Mark introduced himself and spoke consoling words to the couple. He discussed services and support that would be available to them in the months to come.

And so, it went for Mark Walker. On average, Mark would see three to six mothers or couples per day who had lost a child at or before birth. Thursday evenings, from 6:30 to 8:30, Mark led a support group for these mothers and couples. Once a month he also led a support group for women struggling with the fact that they had aborted their child. Many times, abortion feels like the way out for young mothers-to-be, who for one reason or another have made the decision that they are not ready or fit to have a baby. Sometimes the pregnancy is due to rape, but more often it was an unexpected outcome of two willing adults. Unfortunately, abortion for many of these women turned out to be anything but easy.

Today was Thursday and Mr. and Mrs. Smith were his last patients for the day. He finished with the couple by urging them to come to tonight's support group meeting.

"Margaret…Jeffrey… the most effective part of the healing process is to talk about how you feel with others who have gone through similar experiences. If you are uncomfortable expressing your feelings tonight, you can just listen to the others. There is also a lot of healing that takes place just by listening and realizing that there are people who feel similar to the way that you feel."

Mark paused for a moment and let what he said sink in. "Can I count on seeing you two there?" Both Margaret and Jeffrey solemnly nodded their heads yes. "You will be glad you did. I look forward to seeing both of you tonight."

Mark walked out of their hospital room and back towards the nurse's station. There he entered his notes from the discussion into Saint John's computer system. He also entered a reminder in his calendar to follow-up with Mr. and Mrs. Smith by phone in two weeks, which was the standard protocol that he followed with his patients. Oftentimes there is an initial outpouring of support from friends or family, but life soon goes back to normal for everyone else but those who lost their child. Soon the parents, and especially the mother, find themselves dealing with the loss alone. The first few months of grief, before they have made strong connections with others who have experienced similar losses and developed habits for healthy coping skills, are the most crucial. *When a parent dies, you lose your past; when a child dies, you lose your future.* Mark's goal was to give those grieving a future.

Mark looked at his watch. It read 3:32 PM. He had started his work day at 6:30 this morning with a young single mother of two, who lost her third child 16 weeks into her pregnancy. *I still have time to run to the gym before tonight's meeting,* he thought to himself, as he got up to leave Labor and Delivery. He looked over to the nurse who had paged him earlier. "I'll see you later Mindy." "Goodbye Mark. And, no offense, but I hope it won't be too soon." Mark smiled and nodded, "me too," as he walked out the double doors of the department.

After spending some time on the treadmill, Mark showered at the gym and drove to the support group meeting. He pulled into Saint Luke's Presbyterian Hospital Parking Garage at 6:00 PM. St. Luke's is central to the area and had several meeting rooms that he could use for the support groups. Mark set up the room by arranging 16 chairs facing each other in a circle. This was to create an open environment for talking and healing the participants' emotional wounds. He also pulled a foam square rectangle with a wooden handle at one end, out of the bag that he had brought in. This carried the nickname of *The Club*. Mark sometimes had group members, who were feeling angry and frustrated about their loss, use that foam club to hit the iron column at the end of the room. He would tell the others who watched the parent's aggression spew out toward the iron column,

"The mind and the body are linked. Use your body to expel all that anger, hurt and pain your mind has refused to let go. It's not about forgetting, it's about moving forward...taking control of your future." They hit and yelled at the column as hard, loud and as long as they wanted. It usually only lasted about a minute until the participant stopped from exhaustion, but that minute of intense work really helped to ease some of their frustrations.

Jeffrey and Margaret were the first to arrive. "Jeffrey . . . Margaret, I'm glad that you could make it." Soon after their arrival, several more couples came in. They were followed by a few women that came without partners. Six-thirty came and Mark began the meeting.

"Welcome to the support group for families and friends who have lost a child due to a miscarriage, stillborn, or delivery complication. We have some new people in our group. Let's start by introducing ourselves." Everybody in the circle took a turn to stand up and tell the group their name and why they were there.

When that exercise was completed, Mark continued, "Megan, last week you ended our session with *The Club*. Would you like to start us out?" Megan, a 5'7" petite brunette, was one of the single women who had wandered in just as the class was about to start. She was naturally beautiful, but looked exhausted, smelled like smoke and her make-up free eyes were puffy from crying earlier that afternoon.

"How did the loss of your baby, Brandon, make you feel?" Megan slowly stood up and walked over to grab *The Club*. With *The Club* in hand, she walked towards the iron column at the other end of the room and said, "It fucking sucks!" When she reached the column she began hitting, swearing, and crying about the loss of her baby boy, who seemed healthy at birth.

During that first night at the hospital, Megan had fallen asleep with her baby wrapped up tight in a blanket on her chest. She woke up an hour or two later. When she looked down and touched his face, it was cool, but it didn't register at first. "Hey baby," she said softly as she touched his lips. "Hey baby," she said a little louder. Megan sat in shock for a minute. "Oh God. Please no God...Please help. Somebody please help," she said even louder, as tears began to stream down her cheeks. The nurses ran in with the doctor on call following a few seconds later. They worked on baby Brandon, but his heart never beat again. Sudden Infant Death Syndrome (SIDS) was listed as the cause of death, but Megan held onto the thought that her baby's father had wished him to death. He didn't want to have the baggage of a baby as a result of just looking for some random casual sex. He had pushed for an abortion, but Megan would have nothing of it.

Megan eventually calmed down and came back to the circle, flushed red with dots of sweat on her forehead. That night everyone, including Jeffrey and Margaret, shared their feelings and cried with the group. At 8:30 PM, the members of the support group hugged each other and left to deal with their losses on their own, but more connected than they had been before attending the meeting that night.

The Saturday meeting, which came around once a month, was the most difficult for Mark. People generally have an easier time getting to the point to accept the fact that some babies are just not meant to be on earth at this time, despite all we do to try to get them here. Abortions were a different matter. Nobody really knows when life actually starts. When does the spirit enter the body? If the spirit doesn't have the opportunity to visit this body, will it be able to enter another? There are books of arguments and discussions on both sides of the topic. The more recent technology with imaging and monitoring of brainwaves at very early stages can be quite compelling or feel quite damning to some, but Mark refrained from taking a stance on either side of the controversy. There was never any judgement in Mark's support groups. By the time women made their way to him, the choice had already been made. His purpose was to prevent the loss of another life, either mentally, through divorce, through drugs and alcohol, or sometimes by suicide, when these would-have-been mothers could not shake the grief, guilt or even shame placed upon them by others or themselves. Religious philosophy and societal shunning played a number on these women emotionally. Many abortion clinics also did a terrible job at really explaining what actually occurs.

Saturday's session started at 9:00 AM. There were usually between 10 and 15 people who attended the session; however, Mark did notice that more and more people seemed to be attending lately, to the extent that he was considering a second class. Those who attended this class were all women. Their emotional states were a lot more fragile than the support group on Thursdays. Two women, who sporadically attended the abortion support meetings last year killed themselves about a month apart.

Lorena was a light skinned, full-bodied 17-year-old girl with strawberry blond hair. Passion took hold of her the beginning of her senior year in high school when her boyfriend got her pregnant after they snuck away during a high school dance. Lorena had always made him use protection, but this time she didn't press the issue when the moment came. Six weeks later when she confirmed her pregnancy and told her boyfriend through tears, he had pressured her hard into aborting the baby. "We can't do this. It will ruin our lives and my chance to play football in college." First she refused, but eventually Lorena wore down and succumbed to the abortion. She never forgave herself. During the support groups she spoke about the flashbacks she continued to have of her lying back with her feet in the stirrups, feeling the pressure and digging going on inside, while being unable to look down at what was happening to her body.

One year to the day, while home alone, Lorena entered her parents' room. She walked straight to her father's bedside drawer where she took out his Smith and Wesson 357 magnum revolver he kept there for protection. She put the gun in a small backpack and walked down two blocks from her house to a wilderness trail area. After walking about a half mile up a dirt trail, she left the trail and walked through the trees to a spot where she and the boy who got her pregnant used to meet sometimes late at night. After missing for two days, her parents reached out to the would-have-been-father, frantic and worried about their daughter. Panic and a fear of what he suspected shot through her ex-boyfriend. If she had done something drastic, he knew where she would be. When he visited this meeting place, he found her body leaned up against a boulder with half of her head spread against the large rock she had sat against.

The second woman was in her thirties. She was 5'2" and Hispanic with black hair. Despite her Catholic upbringing, she had gone through three abortions by the time she began attending the meetings. She had started to drink more and more in the months preceding her death. Mark could see that he was losing her, but no matter what he said or did, he didn't seem to be able to get through. Eventually she stopped showing up. Mark left messages before each meeting that were never returned. A golfer that sliced one of his drives into the rough, found her body hanging lifeless from one of the trees that lined the golf course just a mile from the apartment building she had lived in.

Chapter 3

Three years later

Professor Walker concluded the first day of his course on *Sociology of Social Problems* by stating, "I quote Ivan Pavlov in saying, 'Don't become a mere recorder of facts, but try to penetrate the mystery of their origin.' And thus that, in no more words, sums up our focus for this semester." As the students gathered their things and walked towards the classroom exit, professor Walker stopped two of his students. "Stephanie, Malcolm, can I speak to you for a moment?" Both stopped to stand by Professor Walker's podium, as they waited for the other students to exit. "I don't have time to discuss it now before my next class, but I would love to speak to both of you later this afternoon about a project I've been considering. Are you available later?"

"My last class ends at 1:30 today," Stephanie said.

"I'm available at 2:00," Malcolm said.

"Two o'clock it is. Can you meet me at my office then?" Both agreed and left to their next class.

Just before 2:00 PM, Malcolm saw Stephanie walking towards the Sociology Building. "Hey Steph! Wait up." Malcolm jogged over to Stephanie and they walked the rest of the way to the office of Professor Walker. Malcolm was an African American student at the University of Denver (DU). He was 5'10", average build, with his hair cut short. He had been born in Ogden, an old railroad city in the northern part of Utah, but had moved to Colorado with his mother, older sister, and younger brother his sophomore year in high school. After graduating high school in Colorado Springs, Malcolm moved 100 miles north to Denver where he attended college and was now just starting his senior year.

Stephanie was 5'6" with fair complexion and dark brown hair that stopped right below her shoulders. She moved to Colorado three years prior to attend school, ensuring that she was able to get a good seven hours away from the small central Utah town she had grown up in. The only real difficulty about leaving Marysvale, Utah was that she was away from her father. Stephanie grew up being especially close with her dad. He never had any boys to hunt and fish with, but Stephanie filled that role well and spent a lot of time walking through fields and embarking on early morning hikes up the Monroe Mountain Range. Stephanie was also a senior at DU. Both she and Malcolm had known each other for a couple of years with a common major in Sociology.

Professor Walker's office door was open when they approached. "Hi Professor Walker," Stephanie said.

Mark Walker looked up at Malcolm and Stephanie. "Hi. Come on in. Please sit."

Professor Walker then looked back at his computer screen and finished what he had been working on before they arrived. After finishing his last key stroke, he stared off into another area of the room and seemed lost in thought.

"What was it you wanted to talk to us about?" asked Stephanie.

Professor Walker looked back at Stephanie and Malcolm, smiled apologetically and said, "I would like you and Malcolm to work with me on a project, in place of your other class requirements. Would you be willing to work with me on something outside of the core curriculum?"

"Tell us more," answered Malcolm. Both Stephanie and Malcolm were top Sociology students within the program. Mark, a.k.a. Professor Walker, had met them as he began teaching ad-hoc classes in behavior and sociology the year before, which gave him a much needed release from his work at the surrounding hospitals consoling those who had lost a child to death.

"I have noticed a trend of decreased emotion," Professor Walker said. "I first began to notice it in my support groups, but it really seems to be happening much more throughout society in general. I would like you two to find out why that is. It will take a lot of work, but I think it will also be very rewarding if you are able to get down to the core of what's happening. What do you think?"

"Okay, but that topic sounds a little broad; where do you recommend we start?" asked Stephanie.

"What I would like to do is give you an outline of the changes that I have noticed happening. Find out reasons why the changes on that list seem to have occurred. When you find other trends relating to this topic, add them to the list. Is that fair?"

"I'm game," said Malcolm.

"Then I'm in too," said Stephanie.

"Good. Let's plan on talking in my office next week at the same time?"

"Sounds like a plan," answered Malcolm.

Stephanie nodded her head and said, "Sure. I look forward to it."

Chapter 4

One week later

Malcolm and Stephanie met just outside of the building where Professor Walker had his office.

"Have you given much thought to our assignment, Steph?" asked Malcolm.

"A little, and there does seem to be something, doesn't there?"

"Yea, there does. What have you found?"

Stephanie said, "I watched my nephew this weekend while my sister was in town. I had to take him to the doctor's office for an earache. When I got there, it just seems like kids were in much worse shape than they should have been for just coming into the office."

"What do you mean?"

Stephanie elaborated, "It may have just been a bad day, but the kids seemed to be really sick. The parents didn't seem to be worrying like I would expect, and they seemed to be disengaged from what their kids were doing. Many of the kids were crying or fighting with others. The parents didn't even say anything to them about it. Things like that never would have happened when we grew up."

"Well that's what happens when you take him to the Hood to see the doctor," replied Malcolm with a smirk.

"That's just it. It's an upper-middle-class area."

There was a pause as they both thought about it, then Malcolm said, "Since we got this assignment, I've noticed things like that too. I don't know if it is just how society has changed what's important, or what it is."

"Well, I guess we're going to need to find that out, aren't we?"

Malcolm nodded in agreement.

As they reached Professor Walker's office, they saw him sitting behind his wooden desk reading papers. The professor looked up as he heard them approach. "Come on in. Please sit." Malcolm and Stephanie both walked in and sat down in the two chairs opposite the side of the desk where Professor Walker sat. Professor Walker looked at each of them. "Are you two still up for this assignment?"

"Yes," Malcolm replied, "in fact, we were just talking about how we've been noticing the change."

"Good. Let's get to work then."

Professor Walker pulled out two copies of an outline that he had put together and handed a copy to Stephanie and Malcolm.

There wasn't much to the outline beyond a title and a list of places to start looking into.

"Project Caffeine?" inquired Malcolm. "I thought this was supposed to be on emotional loss."

"Exactly," answered Professor Walker. "You two are going to find out why society is becoming more apathetic and what we can do to correct this problem. You two are the caffeine that will awaken society from this emotional slumber we find ourselves in."

As they all looked at the outline in more detail, the list of items cited as suffering from emotional loss included:

- Abortion without remorse. . . on the increase
- Emotional numbness with child loss
- Public disengagement from politics
- Superficial self-interest increased
- Willing to sacrifice long-term goals for short term pleasures

Professor Walker instructed his two students, "Here are the general changes that I have personally noticed. I don't want to give you much more specifics than what I have listed here, because I don't want to bias your research or the direction that you take with this project. Obviously, you are going to have to find out why this is happening before you can determine how to fix it. You will have until the end of the semester to have your theory and solution ready to present. How does that sound?"

"It sounds like a lot to figure out within a semester," Malcolm said.

"It will take a significant amount of effort. I recognize that. At the same time, this is something that could really set you apart from your peers within the Sociology Department. This project is more in line with what some may do for their doctoral dissertation. There's a reason why I picked you two. I believe you can find something significant behind what's going on."

Stephanie and Malcolm let what the professor said sink in. "Well, let's do it," Malcolm said.

"I'm up for the challenge, too, Professor," Stephanie added.

"Excellent. Well, get out and get to the bottom of what's going on," Professor Walker said smiling.

Malcolm and Stephanie walked from Professor Walker's office a little overwhelmed with the ambiguity of the class assignment and the grade that would follow.

"Where do you think we should start?" asked Malcolm.

"I think that the best place to start is the library. Let's find out who else has documented this change? Is there a certain point where the changes become more prevalent? And, are there other areas that are affected?" answered Stephanie.

"What are you doing tomorrow afternoon," asked Malcolm.

"I finish my last class at 3:30," said Stephanie.

"Shall we make it a date?"

"I'll see you then."

Stephanie and Malcolm went their separate ways. Later that evening Stephanie took her clothes to her apartment laundromat. While pouring bleach into her whites, a news story on the 24-inch TV at one end of the room caught her attention. "A nine-year-old boy was mauled this morning by three coyotes in the Denver suburb of Erie, Colorado."

Chapter 5

Shortly after 3:30 PM, Stephanie walked into the library where she saw Malcolm at one of the computers.

"Hey, what's up Steph?" asked Malcolm as he saw her approach.

"Hey Malcolm. Find anything good?"

"Not yet, I'm just getting started. How are you doing? How's class?"

"They're okay." Stephanie paused for a moment, then continued, "It's really weird, but the more this project is on my mind, the more and more I see how people have changed."

"Fill me in."

"Did you watch the local news last night?"

"No."

"Well there was a kid who was mauled to death by coyotes yesterday."

"So you're saying it's affecting coyotes too? They just need the fear of man put back in them. I've got an AR-15, decked out to be the ultimate coyote killing machine. It's perfect for the job!"

"No it's not the coyotes," Stephanie said as she hit him on the shoulder. "It's the parents."

"It'll probably work on them too," Malcolm replied with a smirk.

"Ha, Ha. No, this is serious Malcolm. It's horrible what happened to that boy, and what really bothers me is the way the parents acted towards their son's death."

Malcolm got more serious, "I was just playin. Sorry. So, how did they act?"

"They definitely weren't happy, but they didn't act as sad or angry as I would expect someone to act that just had their son mauled to death."

Going back to taking jabs at Stephanie, Malcolm sarcastically said, "I know you're only a fourth-year sociology student, but people do respond to grief differently. They were probably in shock."

"Maybe, but it seemed different."

Over the next few hours they researched library databases and internet sources around their topics.

"Look at this Malcolm."

"You're still looking at news?"

"The papers and networks that focus on traditional headlines, like crime and politics, have decreased in followership every year for the last 5 years. Networks that tailor to shows that are primarily for pleasure, like *Entertainment Tonight* and *The Bachelor*, have increased viewership and revenue continually over the last 5 years."

"The only news station that continues to do well is CNS (Central News System)," said Malcolm as he looked down the list Stephanie was looking at. "What's odd is that CNS is actually more news and politics than the others. It's also more bold, with more polarizing topics."

After several hours, they had expanded their list of impact to the sociological phenomenon they were researching to the following, comparing the current 5-year period to the previous 5-plus year history:

- News and Politics down, except CNS
- Decreased political engagement
- Welfare and Food Stamps have continued to increase over the last 5 years
- Petty Theft is up, Murder is down
- National Student Competency Test grades have decreased every year for the last 4 years
- College and University attendance is down

"Well this gives us a start," Malcolm commented. "I think we should probably dive into each of these. Do you want to focus on finding reasons for the first 3 and I'll focus on the second?"

"Sure, and let's both just keep an eye out for a general loss of emotion."

Stephanie looked down at a text that had just come in on

her cell phone. *Call me asap.* "Excuse me for a minute. It's my dad. I need to call him."

"Sure. I think we're about finished for today anyways. I'll clean up."

Stephanie dialed her father's cell phone as she walked out of the library. A couple of minutes later Malcolm stepped out into the front library entryway to see Stephanie talking on the phone with tears running down her face.

Malcolm looked with wide eyes as she looked towards him. He mouthed, "Are you okay?" She shook her head no and finished the conversation with her dad. "What's wrong Steph?"

"It's my mom. She's in the hospital. I've got to go to Utah."

That night Stephanie packed some clothes for the trip in a small suitcase and drove through the mountainous range on Interstate 70, stretching between Colorado and Utah. About 8 hours later, Stephanie arrived at the Richfield community hospital where her mother had been admitted.

It was a small town hospital that did not have all of the amenities or the expertise of the larger hospitals in the Salt Lake Valley, but it was much better than any small clinic available in the town of Marysvale, where her parents and sister were still living. Stephanie rushed in through the front of the hospital. Inside she saw an elderly woman at a front desk with a sign reading *Information.* "Hi I'm here to see Maryann Petersen. She's in the ICU. I'm her daughter."

After receiving information that the ICU and her mother were on the second floor, Stephanie quickly made her way to the elevators, which were located across the hall from the information desk. When she got in, Stephanie pressed 2, and waited as the elevator doors slowly shut and just seemed to inch up to the second level. As the elevator door opened on the second floor, she saw her father sitting, with his head down, on a padded bench that was located to the right of a large door with a sign above it reading *Intensive Care Unit.* He looked up. His face had a look of defeat, eyes were swollen and tears wet his face. When he saw Stephanie, he just shook his head.

"Oh my God, Dad!" All of Stephanie's worst thoughts were spiraling through her mind and poured out on her face like a faucet of tears. "Where's mom?"

"I'm sorry sweetheart. We lost her."

Chapter 6

Malcolm lived with two other African American college students in a 3-bedroom apartment across the street from the University of Denver. Malcolm was considered the nerd of the group, with each of his roommates attending the University on football scholarships. Reggie Wilson at 5'10" tall and 210 lbs. was one of the two starting running backs his junior year and was returning with high expectations to complete his last year of eligibility. Cliff Patterson was also a senior at the University and towered over both Malcolm and Reggie with height and mass at 6'7", tipping the scales at 340 lbs. He played left offensive tackle and had obtained significant interest from several professional teams. Malcolm and Reggie each helped Cliff with school, where he often bordered on maintaining the marks needed to continue his eligibility to play. Although he physically dominated the line, he struggled academically, which is why he attended the University of Denver instead of many Division 1 teams he had originally aspired to play for. Despite his academic struggles, he was in line to make more money with the pros than either Reggie or Malcolm in their future careers.

Each room in their furnished apartment had a twin sized bed, a closet, wooden brown painted dresser drawers, and matching desk with a small white-shaded lamp. At home, Malcolm continued his research through the internet on a personal laptop. He spent hours Googling different terms of apathy, indifference, and loss of passion. He skimmed through different articles and websites with nothing really catching his eye. It soon became late, and Malcolm's eyes were tired from looking at the computer screen. He changed into some old gym shorts to get ready for bed then walked out to their shared bathroom and brushed his teeth.

"You still studying?" yelled Cliff from the couch in the central living room.

"Yeah, and you better too, if you're going to play for us this year."

"I don't got to study. I got you bro!" Both he and Reggie were watching a football game on TV.

"Get a beer and come watch the game with us," said Reggie.

"Okay," Malcolm replied.

"Really?" Cliff said, as he took his eyes off the TV to look at Malcolm standing in the doorway of his bedroom.

"Yeah. I haven't had one beer in the year and a half you've known me, but yes, let's get blasted," Malcolm said sarcastically.

"See Maw, studying won't do this man any good," Reggie said, poking at Cliff. Maw was a nickname both Reggie and Cliff called Malcolm. It came from his initials M.W. and his motherly nagging to clean up the place and get to studying. They all laughed and Malcolm went back into his room and shut the door. Malcolm hopped in bed and picked up his scriptures to read before going to sleep, which had been his routine since the winter of his senior year of high school. He opened the book and began reading. A light bulb illuminated in his mind as he read across a verse that said, "And others will he pacify, and lull them away into carnal security that they will say: All is well in Zion; yea, Zion prospereth, all is well—and thus the devil cheateth their souls, and leadeth them away carefully down to hell." He jumped up to his computer and typed "lull" into the search engine.

Chapter 7

Back at the hospital, Stephanie sat with her father, Mike Petersen.

"Where's Mom?"

"She's still inside," her father answered as he gestured towards the ICU. "I was there when she passed and already said my goodbye. I came out to give Kathy a minute with Mom before they took her away."

There was a pause in their conversation as Stephanie internalized what was happening. "I'm going in to see Mom. Hang in there, Dad. I'm here for you," Stephanie said as she wiped tears from her face and stood up to walk into the ICU.

When Stephanie walked into the room where her mother lie, Kathy's back was to her. Stephanie slowly walked up, tears again streaming down her face, and put her arms around Kathy. When Stephanie loosened her hug, Kathy turned around and looked at Stephanie. No tears were coming from Kathy's eyes.

Chapter 8

When Malcolm typed "lull" into his search engine, as with the other searches, many things came up, ranging from the definition of *lull*, people with the last name of Lull, and the "lull before a storm." After advancing through many lists of web pages, Malcolm found something of interest to him. He clicked on the link reading, "Emotional lull caused from flu-shot administration." As he followed this link it lead to a clinical abstract from the Journal of American Medical Association (JAMA).

It focused on disputing the previous research by a professor of Internal Medicine out of Stanford University named Edward Temkin, who claimed that flu shots caused an emotional lull in 85% of those who had obtained one, starting back as early as 2007. Professor Temkin stated that an agent that began to be utilized to stabilize the vaccine in 2007 had a negative neurologic impact on laboratory rats that it was administered to. The article, written and authored by two scientists from the Food and Drug Administration, went on to state that the research had been flawed due to the condition that the rats were kept in. It also discussed chemical differences between rat subjects and human subjects, stating that even if the rat conditions had been optimized, the correlation between the impact on rats and humans could not be substantiated and that current flu vaccine formulations were safe and recommended for administration to all humans, starting at age 5, to avoid flu epidemics within the school system and general society.

Malcolm scrolled down to the footnotes and found the reference to Professor Temkin's original article. Malcolm searched for the article and then subscribed to obtain access to the Archives of Internal Medicine, where it was published. When he searched the journal given in the reference, the article had been removed from the online publication.

Malcolm continued his search by typing "Edward Temkin, Stanford" into the search engine. Multiple links to articles popped up. Malcolm learned that Professor Temkin had been an acclaimed professor and had won the prestigious Scientific Innovation Award in 1995 for his work on identifying new targets to neutralize resistant strains of Community Acquired Pneumonia. He was also listed as a contributing investigator to the working group established by the FDA to develop a more effective flu vaccine. Several months after his appointment to this special working group, Edward Temkin lost his place as a member of the Flu Vaccine Optimization working group, which was established in 2006. In 2008, Professor Temkin published the article titled "Emotional Lull Caused from Flu-shot Administration." Three months after the publication, he was fired from Stanford School of Medicine for ethical misconduct and for utilizing inappropriate laboratory and testing techniques with his research.

Malcolm scrolled further down the original search page and found a newspaper article on Abraham Temkin. The son of Edward and Maria Temkin was killed tragically in an anti-Semitic hate crime. He had been beaten to death by a sect of the Aryan Nation. A cross was then placed in the front yard of the Temkin residence and set to fire, as a symbolic retaliation for the crucifixion of Jesus Christ. Abraham Temkin was survived by his parents and younger sister, Ruth.

Malcolm logged onto an online background check company to try to determine what happened to Edward Temkin after this incident. After entering his credit card number to obtain his report, he found multiple addresses and information indicating a divorce from his wife, Maria. The current address on the report for Edward was 1742 East Monroe Parkway in Oakland, California.

Chapter 9

Stephanie said a tearful goodbye to her mother who had died from an infection that was caused by a complication from a botched removal of her appendix. Months earlier the surgeon had inadvertently nicked her intestine while performing the procedure and went on to sew her up with the intestine leaking waste and bacteria into her abdomen. While recovering at home in the weeks post-surgery, the infection spread and Stephanie's mother grew sick.

Grief-stricken, Stephanie left the hospital and began the thirty-minute drive to her parent's home to await the funeral. Kathy and Stephanie's father, who came up to Richfield with a friend, rode back to Marysvale with Stephanie. Kathy lived with her husband and 9-year-old son next door to her parents' house. There was not a lot of talking that occurred on the way home, besides some awkward and out-of-place comments by Kathy.

"If we hurry, we can get back in time to see who Jim picks on *The Bachelor*," Kathy said. Stephanie kept silent with her hands on the wheel and just shook her head. Her father, who sat directly behind her, placed a hand on Stephanie's shoulder and placed his head against the back of her seat. He remained there until they arrived in Marysvale.

Once inside her childhood home and alone with her father, Stephanie asked, "Dad, what's going on with Kathy?"

"Everyone deals with loss differently."

"Maybe, but not like that. I haven't even seen her shed one tear. How long has she been acting like this?"

"If I recall, you and Kathy have never really seen eye to eye."

"Not on everything, but where we disagree, it's always been passionate for each of us. It's like she's lost her emotions."

Stephanie's father sat silent for what seemed to be a long while. As Stephanie studied her father's face, she could see pain and struggle emerging beneath the wrinkles the years had brought him.

"Both she and your mother have been acting that way for a little over a year. To be honest, it's been hard. I felt like I was losing your mother long before this happened."

"When did you notice the change Dad?"

Her father leaned his head back and looked at the ceiling as he thought for a moment. "It started happening last spring. We used to go for walks every morning together with Jasper." Jasper was their 11-year-old Border Collie.

"Little by little, she stopped wanting to go. She eventually got out of the habit from doing anything with Jasper or me. She just set herself in front of that damn TV, either ours or Kathy's." There was a brief pause before he continued, "and Drake has become even more worthless than when your sister married him." There had been long-standing tension between Mike and his son-in-law. Drake had grown up locally and, according to Mike, never really showed much ambition. Mike had tried to convince his daughter that she deserved better, until Kathy's pregnancy further solidified their relationship and their choice to marry shortly after.

"What about Nathan?" Nathan was Kathy's 9 year old son.

"Besides his parents paying no *good* attention to him, he's good. He and I have been buddies through all of this. To be honest, he's what's kept me going. He needs me right now. He wouldn't even be getting to school half the time if I wasn't right here." Almost on cue, Nathan came running through the back screen door.

"How's Grandma?" Mike pat the couch right beside him and Nathan sat down next to his grandpa. As Nathan sat beside his grandfather, silence filled the room. The appropriate words just didn't seem to come to Mike.

"What's wrong?" asked Nathan.

"Grandma went to Heaven honey."

A look of anguish appeared on Nathan's face as the tears welled up in his eyes. Mike pulled him close to him. Stephanie moved closer, with Nathan between her and her father, and put an arm around both of them. They embraced and all cried together.

Chapter 10

As Reggie and Cliff walked into their apartment, Malcolm could hear them talking about their upcoming game. "Where's St. Francis again?" asked Cliff.

"It's in Emeryville," answered Reggie.

"Ok. Where the hell is Emeryville?"

"By Oakland numbnut."

"Why should I know that nappi-ass?"

Malcolm interrupted from the couch in their front room, "You guys are playing in Oakland this Friday?"

"No, we're playing St. Francis Christian College, in Emeryville, near Oakland," answered Cliff, while giving Reggie dirty looks.

"You should come Maw, so you can watch us whoop the ass of your Christian brotherhood!" taunted Reggie.

"I just might," Malcolm replied

Early Thursday morning, Malcolm stopped by the Quick Trip corner gas station and got a Vanilla Coke and sunflower seeds to keep him occupied for the long drive ahead. According to MapQuest, it was going to take him 17 hours and 23 minutes to get to Oakland from Denver. He had reserved a room near the address of Professor Temkin.

About 2 hours into the drive, Malcolm was jolted out of his daze by bright rear tail-lights quickly approaching in front of him. He slammed on the breaks, not sliding, but stopping quickly about 3 feet from the rear of the black Toyota pickup truck in front of him. Stopped in front of the Toyota truck, was a blue Jeep, a silver hatchback and white sedan. Malcolm couldn't see if there were any more, with the road bending around the large protruding mountainside.

A few moments later the cars started moving again. From what he could tell, none of the cars had hit each other. As he made the turn around the mountain edge, all three cars in front of him pulled over on the gravel turnout to the right of them. Malcolm slowly drove by staring at the cars. A brunette woman stepped out of the black Toyota truck. She looked at Malcolm driving slowly around her. She put her hand next to the right side of her face with her thumb up and little finger down, making the gesture of a phone and mouthed, "call 911." She looked away as Malcolm passed and he could see in his rearview mirror as she ran across the canyon road where she stopped to look over the edge of a ravine.

Malcolm pulled his Dodge Journey off to the side in front of the black truck. After placing his vehicle in park, he ran across the road. As he approached he followed the gaze and finger pointing down the ravine where he saw a sedan lying upside down in the middle of the river that was located at the bottom of the ravine. The driver's side was completely smashed in, facing upstream and filling with water. The passenger side was not as crumpled. The windows on the passenger side remained intact and that side tilted slightly up out of the water where it rested on one of the boulders in the river. Two wheels had been ripped off the sedan. As Malcolm moved his eyes to the riverbank and up the side of the ravine the sedan had traveled down, he could see one tire on the shore next to the river, with the other halfway up the ravine.

Malcolm began quickly climbing down the ravine to the river's edge. People lined the roadway that he had just come from. There were also people beginning to accumulate near the water's edge, who appeared to have come from a hiking path near the riverbank. No one had entered the water. As Malcolm arrived at edge of the water, he asked a small group of people near him if anyone was alive. A young thin white man with long dirty blond dreadlocks pointed and said, "he's moving." Malcolm looked back to the sedan and could see that something was moving inside the car. He waded straight into the water. The cold temperature was not much above freezing and it sent a shock through his body as it soaked through his jeans. The water did not appear to be moving too quickly, yet when Malcolm moved further in, he struggled to keep his footing against the pressure of the river and the loose rocks below him.

Malcolm made his way to the passenger side of the car, which was downstream and still primarily out of the water. He tried to pull open the passenger door, but it would not budge. The lower half of the man inside was positioned in the driver's seat, with the upper part of his body lying towards the passenger side of the car. Water was quickly filling up the space. It was difficult to tell, but it looked like the man was still strapped into his seat belt. His eyes, full of fear, met Malcolm's.

"Is anyone else in there?" Malcolm yelled. The man shook his head no. He had dirty grey hair, an untrimmed beard, and had a green stocking hat resting halfway off his head. This man was bleeding from his left cheek bone, but it was difficult to see if there was any injury beyond that. The water that kept filling the cab, seemed to accelerate. At this rate, it would soon go over the man's head. Malcolm looked around for a rock, but everything nearby was too large to pick up. He reached in his pocket and pulled out his Leatherman multi-tool.

"Cover your eyes," Malcolm yelled to the driver. The man inside the car closed his eyes. Malcolm stepped back and hit the side window with all that he had. The glass shattered and water ran over the now clear window space, which provided some relief for the stranded man.

"Can you undo your seatbelt?" The man just shook his head no. Malcolm could now see the man visibly shaking. If the water didn't overtake him, hypothermia would. The driver's face was very pale. Malcolm noticed a pink stream of water that came from somewhere below the water line. Malcolm unlocked the passenger door and was able to pull it open. He knelt onto the passenger seat of the car. The water in the car was much lower now and just filled up to the bottom of the seat. Malcolm looked down at the situation the driver was in. It was much worse than he had thought. At the level of the man's belly button, the driver's side door appeared to have folded in and nearly cut him in half.

"Can you move your legs?" Malcolm asked.

This is the first time that he heard the man speak. "No. I can't move anything below my waist."

Malcolm glanced out of the car towards the riverbank and saw a crowd of probably 30 people. Malcolm was still the only person who had even ventured into the water to help. *The Bystander Effect*, Malcolm thought to himself. He had studied horrible scenarios of criminal acts that had taken place with hundreds of people around, yet nobody helped. During sociology class, one particular real scenario influenced Malcolm to commit to himself that regardless of what could happen to him, he would help anyone in need that could not or did not know how to help themselves. He remembered learning of a woman in the New York subway system who was forced by knifepoint to perform oral sex on a man. This was during a peak time, with a lot of pedestrians around. After the sexual assault, he beat her for 30 minutes without one person intervening to stop the horrible crime. He eventually went to prison, but not until after his victim had been slowly beaten to death.

This situation Malcolm found himself in was different. He had acted to save the man, but the reality of what was happening began to sink in for Malcolm. There was no way that this man was getting out of his car alive.

"The paramedics are coming and they will take care of everything in just a couple of minutes," Malcolm said in an attempt to comfort the man. Almost on cue, Malcolm could see the flashing lights at the top of the canyon. "Do you have other family that will need to be notified?"

"I just have one daughter, but I don't think she'd miss me much," the man said while he managed a slight smile.

"My name is Malcolm. What's your name?"

"I'm Reuben Wright."

"Where does your daughter live Reuben?"

"She lives in California with her husband and 2 children."

"What's her name?"

"Synthia Dobson."

"I'm sure that she cares. . . more than you know, Reuben."

"I guess it's probably too late to find out if that's true," Reuben said, as he looked down at where the car crumpled on and into him. "I'm not going to make it, am I?"

Malcolm sat silent for a moment. "I don't know, Reuben."

"Will you do me a favor?"

"What is it?"

"Will you tell my daughter that I'm sorry? I acted like an idiot. My pride just wouldn't let me admit it until now."

"What happened Reuben?"

"Richard, her husband, isn't white. When and where I grew up, races just didn't mix. I was wrong." Reuben paused for a moment, then continued, "it's ironic that the only man that came to my rescue was you--a black man." He paused again, then finished with, "I'm sorry." Just then four paramedics made it to the car. Malcolm began to get out of the cab to make room for them.

"Promise me, Malcolm."

Malcolm turned back and looked into Reuben's eyes. "I promise Reuben."

Malcolm didn't wait around to give a statement to the authorities. He was upset and didn't know what to think about what had just happened. He got back into his Dodge and began driving towards California again.

Chapter 11

After crying together, Stephanie and her father tucked Nathan into his grandparents' queen bed. They both lay by him, one on each side. Stephanie looked around the room as she lay by her nephew. Nothing had changed since she had lived there. In front of the bed stood a large walnut dresser with a mirror. On top of the dresser was a tray where her father kept keys, spare change, and anything random he had happened to put in his pockets during the day. On the east side of the bedroom, the moon shone through the sheer curtains. Outside she could see the outline of the treadmill which still collected dust.

"Dad, should I go tell Kathy?"

Nathan answered for his grandfather, "She doesn't care if I'm here."

"I'll just walk over there so she won't worry," said Stephanie.

"She won't be worried either. It's fine," Nathan said.

Stephanie got up anyway and walked over to Kathy's house. She entered without knocking. Kathy sat on her family room couch and remained fixated on the TV.

"Have you spoken to Nathan about Mom?"

"Um, not yet."

"We let him know."

"Oh, thanks."

"Do you even care how your son is doing?"

"How is he doing?"

"He's taking it hard, unlike you. Do you even care?"

"Steph, I don't have time for this," Kathy said annoyed.

"How do you not have time? Too busy watching TV? What the hell are you doing? Wake up Kathy!"

"If you're going to be a bitch, will you do it after my show?"

"Screw you Kathy!" Stephanie stomped over and turned off the TV. "Don't you EVER call me a bitch! Do you understand me?"

"I'm sorry Stephanie," said Kathy without much emotion. "What would you like to talk about?" Stephanie shook her head in disgust and walked out of the house. On her way back to her parents' house she stopped and looked back at Kathy's place. The TV was back on.

Stephanie sat outside her parents' house and collected herself for a moment before going in. Nathan did not need to see her upset like this towards his mother. When Stephanie walked in, her father was slowly closing his bedroom door.

"How's your sister doing?"

Stephanie rolled her eyes. "I can't believe what's going on with her. How can you deal with it?"

"Do I have a choice?" and there was a pause, "I do it for Nathan. I'm all he has right now." Stephanie walked over to her dad and they hugged for several minutes.

"Come out on the porch with me Steph." Stephanie followed her father out the front door to the screened-in veranda where they each sat in a chair facing the front yard. Mike lit a cigarette and took a long drag. "You're smoking again, Dad?" Mike blew the smoke out and inhaled another drag of his cigarette.

"You know what's funny?" Mike was now looking down at his cigarette. "I've been smoking again for about 9 months. You're the first in the family to say anything."

"What's happening to everybody Dad?"

"I don't know. I wish I did." Just as he spoke, a mosquito abatement truck drove by the house spewing malathion from both sides. Stephanie told her father about the project that she and Malcolm were working on and the trends that they have noticed occurring throughout society.

About 30 minutes later, the mosquito spraying truck drove by again. "It was just over a year ago when your mother and I were sitting out here, just as we are right now. We were close then. In fact, I remember the mosquito truck coming by, just like it did tonight. I remember her saying, 'If that stuff kills mosquitos, what's it going to do to us?'"

"When did they start spraying?"

"It was right about that time."

"Do you think Mom could have been right? Could that stuff have affected her?"

"I don't know, but there was a dream I kept having while all this was going on. In my dream, our entire family is out walking over some of those rolling hills." Stephanie's father gestured out towards the hills in front of them. "Nathan is right next to me. Your mom, Kathy, and Drake are also out there, but they're on the hill just over from the one Nathan and I are on. I see a large black fog moving in. It engulfs Mom, Kathy, and Drake. We can't get to them. The valley is also filled with the black fog. I look the other way and I see you standing upon another hill. The fog is all about you. A large black cloud is moving in about to engulf you...but every night I had that dream, it never does. I always woke before it did. It was the one thing that still gave me hope...that maybe you would make it too and maybe all wasn't lost."

Chapter 12

A little over 16 hours later, Malcolm arrived in Oakland. The area he was driving into was rough. All stores and many of the houses had bars on their windows. Everybody he saw was black. As he turned down another street, it was almost like driving into another country. The Church's Chicken was replaced with Kosher Deli's and a dominant Jewish population. Malcolm pulled into the Palm Motel that sat just outside of the Jewish area. It was already dark and quite late. Malcolm checked in at the front office of the motel, got his key and drove to the parking spot in front of his door.

About 5 doors down from his room, were several college-age black men standing outside their room drinking and laughing. One man looked Malcolm's way. Malcolm nodded at the man, then stepped inside his room, shutting and locking the door. "What am I doing here?" Malcolm said to himself. He set his bag on a chair and typed Dr. Temkin's address into the maps navigation on his phone. He looked at the map and then put the phone in his pocket before opening the door to walk back out to his car. He didn't want anyone here to see that he was not familiar with this area. The lighted GPS on his phone would be a sure sign.

A few minutes later, Malcolm pulled up in front of the professor's small, two-story house. The outside was red and several years overdue for a paint job. There was a narrow driveway on the right side of the front yard with a grass patch down the middle. Malcolm walked up the driveway and then down the concrete path to the steps leading up to the professor's porch and front door. Malcolm knocked. Nobody answered. He waited half a minute then knocked again, harder. Irritation from driving all this way began to set in. He did not come all this way to not visit the professor. Still, there was no sign of anyone stirring within the house.

This time Malcolm pounded on the door. Ten seconds later he saw a light turn on in an upstairs bedroom. A minute later the front door opened slightly. Malcolm could see a chain attached near the top of the door that prevented it from opening any further. "What do you want?" the voice from inside yelled.

"Professor, my name is Malcolm Walker. I've come to talk to you about some of your research."

"There is no professor here," the voice from inside yelled as the door slammed shut. Malcolm knocked hard on the door again.

"Professor, please." Just as Malcolm got those words out, the door flung open and he came face to face with the man pointing a shotgun directly at Malcolm's chest.

"I said, there is NO PROFESSOR HERE!" Malcolm backed away and stumbled down the front porch steps. He walked away from the house in shock by what had just happened. Malcolm shook from adrenaline, felt anger, fear and desperation all mixed together. He passed his car and just kept walking, trying to figure out what to do next. By the time he had settled down a little bit, he was blocks away from the professor's house. He looked at his watch. It was 10:23 PM. He looked closer at his surroundings. Malcolm began to feel a little uneasy with where he was, especially at this time of night. He was dressed a little out of place. He had on a long sleeved, black collared shirt and jeans that looked more preppy than the way the locals dressed in this neighborhood. Not to mention, he was walking these streets alone.

Malcolm turned to go back towards where he had come from. While continuing to scan his surroundings, he saw several people standing around the mouth of an alley between two of the homes. One person started walking towards him. Malcolm kept walking as if he didn't see him. When he got closer, Malcolm could see that it was a black man that looked to be in his twenties. Without even opening his mouth, he reeked of booze.

"Can you spare some change," the man said. He had on a black stocking hat, a black jacket, sweat pants, and tennis shoes.

"I'm sorry man, I don't have any money on me."

"Oh, come on brotha. You gotta have somethin. I don't got no money for food."

"Sorry. I wish I had some," Malcolm said as he continued to walk. He noticed three more figures moving out of the alleyway towards him.

Malcolm had several thoughts running through his mind. Do I run, turn and face him, or just keep walking. On a split decision, Malcolm turned to face the man before the other three got out to where they stood.

"Hey, I don't want any trouble. I told you, I don't have anything."

"You look too pretty for not havin nothin. He looks too pretty, don't he?" the man said to the others approaching. One of the other men then whistled like one would whistle at an attractive woman. Malcolm could see the other three figures more clearly now. All were black men. Two of them looked like they were in their early to mid-20s. The third looked to be in his late teens. The teenager was muscular, wearing a light wife-beater, and had his hair in corn rows. One of the men in his mid-20s was also wearing a white wife-beater and had on a spandex cap. The third man wore an Oakland Raiders ball cap over his spandex skully cap. He had a button up shirt that was undone with a black tee-shirt underneath.

Malcolm knew that if he stayed around, this was not going to end well. He felt that his only real chance was to run, so he turned and ran in the direction of where he thought Professor Temkin's house was. The four men ran after him. Their baggy pants and liquor seemed to give Malcolm an edge. He ran two blocks and turned up another street to try to lose them. After several turns, Malcolm looked around breathing heavily. He seemed to have lost them. Now, he just had to get back to his car. Out of breathe from his run, he walked towards the direction of where he thought his car was.

After 15 more minutes of walking, the panic that had seemed to subside a little, welled up again. He tried to calm himself down by concentrating on breathing deep and slow. He had no idea which way to go. He had already passed where he thought Professor Temkin's house was supposed to be. As Malcolm walked by another alleyway he stopped and kneeled down to pray. He prayed for help in getting out of this mess that he had gotten himself into. He prayed to know which way to go to find his car. He also prayed that his trip here to California wouldn't be in vain.

Malcolm stood up and began walking through the alley he had just been kneeling in. Just as he got near the end, two men walked out of the shadows, blocking his passage through. He recognized them as the guys who tried to get him to stop earlier. Malcolm's body filled with adrenaline and he turned to run. Behind him were the other two men. The man with the Raider's hat said, "Why you look so scared homey?" Malcolm looked towards him and got ready to give all he had to run by or through him and the other man next to him. Almost as if reading his thoughts, the man in the Raider's hat pulled out a gun and pointed it right at Malcolm. "Stay for a while? It's a nice night. You like the night?"

"I don't want any trouble," said Malcolm.

"You got trouble when you lied to us fool." They all closed in on Malcolm. Malcolm felt a punch to the side of his face from someone beside or behind him, which knocked him to the ground. He tried to cover the front of his face, neck, and stomach the best that he could as they all kicked, stomped and hit him. Malcolm heard a large "bang" as everything went black and he lost consciousness.

When Malcolm eventually opened his eyes. Everything was dark. He wasn't in the alley anymore. How long was he out? He stayed motionless, just waiting for his eyes to adjust, searching for clues as to where he was. He was on a bed, and he could make out posts at the end of the bed. There were also patterns, plaid pattern on the curtains in the room he was in. Malcolm's heart nearly jumped out of his chest.

"It can't be," Malcolm thought. "It can't be!" His mind shot back to a summer a long time ago. Malcolm was six years old. His parents had just separated. His mother had gotten a job as a clerk at a local department store to support herself and her children. Some arrangement had been made to have Malcolm's grandmother, on his dad's side, watch him during the day.

Also in the house with Grandma, lived Malcolm's uncle Harold. His mind spun back to the day it started. Malcolm was downstairs playing with a box of matchbox cars. Harold overheard Malcolm playing in the common area outside of his room.

"Malcolm. You wanna watch some cartoons?" his uncle said as he cracked the door open.

"Yeah," answered Malcolm. Harold turned on the TV in his room to a channel with cartoons on it. Harold got in his bed. He was only wearing boxer shorts. "Come hop in bed Malcolm. You can get comfortable in here," his uncle said. He tried to engage Malcolm in simple playful games, where he pretended his fingers were small soldiers marching across Malcolm's body, but Malcolm was more interested in the cartoons to pay too much attention. The finger soldiers marched closer to areas of Malcolm's body that a grown man had no business touching…and that is when it started.

As Malcolm began to get uncomfortable, his uncle made Malcolm feel that he had done something very wrong.

"The way you acted made this happen. You started this game. Now you have to finish the game. After it starts, you can't stop," Harold told Malcolm. Malcolm was hesitant, but fear from what Harold said prompted him to succumb to what was going on.

When this incident ended, Harold made Malcolm promise not to tell anyone. "Your parents would be very mad at you for making me do this."

Malcolm promised and the abuse and the extent of what occurred during the abuse got worse and worse as the days and months of summer went on. Malcolm remembered sitting on the back steps of his grandmother's house as a six-year-old little boy, trying to figure out what to do. Should he tell his mamma? What would she think? What would she do? She was already struggling and Malcolm knew it. He saw her crying in her room many nights. Every night that he saw her crying he stayed up in his room drawing pictures, where he wrote, "I Love You Mom," at the bottom of the page. He wanted her to be happy. He decided that he could not make his mamma any more sad. Nobody could know what Harold had done to him and what he made Malcolm do.

The door opened to the room that Malcolm was in, and he saw a figure standing in the doorway. He jumped out of bed looking for something to fight back with. His vision became tunneled and his head pounded. The light flipped on and the room changed from his uncle's bedroom to an unfamiliar place. In the doorway stood Edward Temkin.

Still fighting to gain his bearings, Malcolm asked, "Where am I?" His balance was off and he put a hand down to steady himself.

"You're in my house. You shouldn't be walking around here this time of night unless you want trouble. Sit down." Malcolm sat on the edge of the bed, his head still pounding.

"What happened?"

"Besides getting your ass kicked?" said the professor with a slight smirk.

"Ah. . . yeah, I remember that part."

"I think the last kick in the head is what put you out."

"What was that bang? Did they shoot?" asked Malcolm. The professor went on to tell him how he heard a commotion and went out to see what was happening. When he saw them beating Malcolm, he fired a shot and they ran. With Malcolm out cold, he carried him into his house to recover.

"Now that you got my attention, what do you want?" asked the professor.

After a few minutes of small talk, to get himself reoriented, Malcolm discussed the articles that he found authored by Professor Temkin.

"Leave it alone Malcolm," warned the professor.

"There's something to it, isn't there? I've come too far. I need answers Professor. Something is going on," said Malcolm.

"This is way over your head son. People have died just being involved in what you are trying to do. It is bigger than you ever imagined. Those guys in the alley are nothing compared to what you are dealing with Malcolm," the professor paused for a moment, then continued, "stop before you get yourself and those around you hurt."

"I'm not stopping Professor. Please let me know what you know." Professor Temkin could see the determination in Malcolm's eyes, and that he was not going to be easily dissuaded from what he was trying to do. Professor Temkin left the room to fix them both a cup of coffee.

When Professor Temkin returned, he offered Malcolm the coffee. "Thank you professor, but I don't drink coffee," said Malcolm.

The professor looked at Malcolm for a moment. "You are

a stubborn kid aren't you," he said with a shake of his head. They both went into the living room where Malcolm sat on the pea green couch across from the matching chair the professor sat in. The professor told Malcolm how he had been a part of the Flu Vaccine Optimization Working Group. The group was tasked with creating a more effective and reliable vaccination against the flu virus. Many strides had been made, including a prospective formulation to stave off the core flu virus, along with the adaptations that occur with the virus year-to-year. Just as those strides were being made, a political appointee from the first cabinet was put in charge of the group. With this appointee came a scientist who brought a formulation that, in his words, "was proven" to stave off the flu virus and promote overall better wellness for the recipients of the vaccine.

The documentation for this new vaccine and the science behind it did not make sense, yet every effort to question the validity of the research was quickly shot down. Dissension around this new compound would not be tolerated. Unsupported by the new head, Michael Wilcox, Professor Temkin took it upon himself to study this compound more thoroughly on laboratory rats during the early morning and after hours. His research indicated a neurologic change in the rats that made them more apathetic than those not given the vaccine. This was shown in the classic rat race, where the first rat through the maze got the cheese at the end.

The treated rats, never won. In fact, they never even came close to the untreated rats. Most never even ventured very far down the maze corridor. When the professor brought his findings to the group, Michael Wilcox immediately fired him, which simultaneously sent a strong message to the rest of the scientists working on the project. The next day, while he was walking back home from the grocery store, where he went to grab some milk for his family, a van pulled up. Two men jumped out of the car and pulled the professor into the van at gunpoint. He was taken to a back alley where he was beaten and warned never to speak a word of his research again. If he did so, the repercussions would be serious.

Professor Temkin returned to his home badly beaten and bloody, yet even more determined to further his research. Over the next year and a half, he furthered his study on animal subjects. When the vaccine was released in 2007, he studied the effects in human subjects. Of the 20 patients he followed with the vaccine over the next year, he reported marked apathy, resulting in job loss, marital problems, obesity, and withdrawal from previously important activities like hobbies, political involvement, voting, family involvement, and community service. Activities that brought immediate satisfaction, like promiscuous sex, alcohol, overeating or drugs also increased in this group. Due to Professor Temkin's reputation and connections within the medical community, he was able to get his data published in a prestigious journal.

After the publication, it was quickly dismantled by several "expert" physicians. One week later, Professor Temkin, his wife and his daughter came home from a dance recital to find flashing lights, a fire truck, and several police cruisers outside his home. On the front lawn was a cross that had been lit on fire. On his front porch was the lifeless body of his teenage son, Abraham Temkin. Carved in the wooden beam near the boy's body, was "Duet. 5:20, 5:7." Professor Temkin knew these scriptures well. They were verses from the Ten Commandments in the old testament. "Thou shalt not bear false witness against thy neighbor" and "Thou shalt have no other gods before me." The officers on the scene had trouble deciphering what this meant. "Why would they inscribe these verses?" he remembered one of the officers saying, but the professor knew exactly what they meant. His exposure of the science "false witness" and his persistence in putting truth above the system "gods before me," were the reasons why his son was killed.

This was too much for his wife Maria to handle. They soon separated and Professor Temkin left their home.

"Did you try to work it out?" asked Malcolm.

"The best thing for me to do, Malcolm, is to stay away from my family. It is the only way I can protect what is left of my family." The professor was crying at this point.

"Don't go any further Malcolm," the professor warned again. "They will not tolerate any leak of what's going on. The people in charge of this can't be touched."

Chapter 13

"Hi Polly."

"Well if you aren't a sight for sore eyes! How have you been Stephanie Petersen?" Pollyanna, the clerk in the Marysvale courthouse exclaimed as she walked over to hug Stephanie.

"Now let me take a look at you. My, my, my. . . you are all grown up." Stephanie couldn't help but smile with Polly's genuine jubilant personality.

"It's good to see you, too, Polly. It looks like you haven't even aged a day. In fact, I think you look younger."

"Oh bless your heart, child." In reality Pollyanna was a slightly overweight 58 year old woman, who had worked in the courthouse ever since Stephanie was alive. With her grey curly hair, wrinkled face, and coffee and tobacco stained teeth, she didn't look a day younger than 60.

"Now, you didn't just come down here to see me did you?" asked Pollyanna.

"Of course I came to see you." Stephanie paused for a

moment, "but since I'm here, I would love to research a couple of things." They both smiled at Stephanie's flattery. After explaining what she was interested in, Pollyanna showed Stephanie the records.

There was a large amount of papers. As she looked through the city records, Stephanie recognized pretty much all of the names of those who had purchased supplies and maintained city property, as well as those who were in charge of different city related responsibilities. It was a small enough town to where most people knew each other. When she found the purchasing records for the mosquito spray used in town, an unfamiliar name was associated with the invoices for the city account.

"Polly, who is Richard Norton?"

Pollyanna said, "Well, that is a good question my dear." She had only spoken to him by phone on one or two occasions.

"Why is he purchasing mosquito spray for Marysvale?"

"A few years ago, the federal mandate came across that any insecticides, fluoride or other additives that could come in contact with people be regulated and maintained by the federal government."

Stephanie wrote down the name and contact information for Richard Norton, thanked Polly, and went home to pack for the trip back to school.

Chapter 14

Malcolm left the professor's house and went to his hotel to sleep the rest of the night and into late morning. He needed a clear head to figure out what to do next. Around 10:00 AM, Malcolm woke covered in sweat. He had been dreaming about his childhood again. This time he was 9 years old. He remembered how he had many sleepless nights, waking up, often from the reoccurring nightmares of the abuse that he had endured just three year before. At 9 years old, years after the abuse, he had still been reliving his hell. Inside, despite the fear and anxiety it brought, he knew he had to eventually tell his parents, who had gotten back together about a year after their separation three years prior. After one of his recurring nightmares, around 3:00 or 4:00 in the morning, he walked into his parents' room crying. This was unlike Malcolm and his mother sat up in her bed concerned.

"What's wrong honey?"

With tears in his eyes, Malcolm told her about what he had endured and the nightmares that continued to haunt him. "I just want them to stop. I'm sorry Momma." His dad was now also awake and sitting up.

"It's not your fault sweetheart. I am so sorry I let this happen to you," and his mom hugged him tight. Malcolm spent that night sleeping between his parents. He slept better that night than he had remembered doing for what had seemed like years, and probably was.

As a result of Malcolm telling his parents, several more cousins admitted to the abuse. Two friends of Malcolm's parents also spoke to their children about unwelcome touching after hearing about what had happened to the Walker son. They discovered that it had been happening to their children as well. One had been abused by an older cousin and the other by a teenage neighbor. After Malcolm had the courage to come forward and to be vulnerable with his parents, the nightmares began to subside. The impact from the positive that happened in others' lives, by his coming forward, made a prominent impression in his mind back then. In fact, he had written about it in his journal. That same impression resonated very strong now. Malcolm knew he had received his answer on what he needed to do. In fact, deep down he always knew. He needed to help those who cannot and do not know how to help themselves. This time, there was even more at stake.

As Malcolm sat up in bed, his head felt like it was about to explode. He slowly got out of bed and shuffled to the bathroom. With the scabs and bruises on his face and body, he looked like he had been through a war. He wasn't going to make the game today looking like that. Besides, he had to get any additional information from the professor that he could. Professor Temkin would not be back home until 1:00 PM, which was after his last class at UC Berkeley where he had been able to land a job after the dismissal from Stanford.

That afternoon, as Professor Temkin pulled up, Malcolm was sitting on the stairs of his front porch. The professor shook his head, but he wasn't surprised. From what he saw the night before, he knew that Malcolm would be there.

"Hi Professor," said Malcolm.

"So you think you have made your decision, have you?" asked Professor Temkin. "Come on in."

The professor fixed both of them a cup of coffee and they sat down in the same chairs they had the night before. Malcolm didn't protest this time and sipped on this hot brew that he hadn't tasted in years. He wasn't exactly sure why, but something was changing in him and he had felt it slowly building within him for a while.

"So why are they doing this Professor?" asked Malcolm.

"Why?...all that I know in regards to why, is that some very powerful people want that formula to be used. They do not care, or in fact, they want the numbing and apathetic effects that do occur," said the professor.

"Are there other medications being used like this?" asked Malcolm.

"It would not surprise me, but I'm not aware of any. I've

stopped aggressively poking around since my son's death."

"Is there anything else that you know that can help me?"

"I do have a few names that I've tracked down of people who are decision makers within the program. I also have some friends that I can trust in the political field. That's the best I can do," said Professor Temkin.

"I'll take it Professor. Thank you."

"Malcolm," the professor said in a very serious tone. "I'm going to say it one more time, even though I don't think it will dissuade you much." He paused for emphasis. "Don't do it. Nothing is below these people. They will do anything to keep their secrets safe."

"I'm already in too deep, Professor."

"Then I will ask one more favor from you. Besides my friends that we can trust, nobody can know that I gave this information to you. Will you promise me that? They will destroy what I have left of my family."

"I promise Professor."

Chapter 15

After leaving Professor Temkin's house, Malcolm pulled into a middle class neighborhood, just a couple of towns over on the East Bay, in Walnut Creek. The house was beige with a single garage and a nicely kept yard. Down the street he saw several children playing street hockey. When he knocked on the door, a white woman, who looked to be in her thirties, answered.

"Hi, are you Mrs. Dobson?" Right then an eight-year-old, light skinned black boy ran by her on his way inside.

"Leave your hockey stick outside Tyson." The stick came flying out of the doorway onto the lawn beside the steps.

"I'm sorry about that. Do I know you?"

"No, you don't. I spoke to your father before he died." Synthia stared at him awestruck.

"I was there when he died."

"Oh my," Synthia said to herself as she looked away. Synthia looked back at Malcolm and into his eyes. He seemed like he genuinely cared. Synthia had trouble reconciling the situation in her mind…a black man coming to speak to her about the death of her racist father. "Please, come in." Synthia opened the door wider, allowing Malcolm to walk inside. She gestured towards the faux leather couch. "Can I get you something to drink? A water perhaps?"

"A glass of water would be great. Thank you," Malcolm replied as he sat on the couch.

Synthia walked to the kitchen. She went out of sight for a moment, and then came back into sight with two glasses that she filled with water from the Culligan water dispenser. She walked back into the front room, offered a weak smile and asked, "Did he tell you why we no longer had a relationship?"

Synthia now sat on the opposite side of the couch with her knee sideways on the cushion so she could face Malcolm as she waited for his response.

"He told me that he was wrong for alienating you and your husband and that he was truly sorry. Those were his last words."

Synthia looked down at her glass while Malcolm continued to study her.

"My dad was right about him being no good." She looked up at Malcolm. "But, not because he's black. He's been gone for almost a year."

"I'm sorry to hear that. I know it's none of my business and you don't know me, but do you mind if I ask what happened?"

"He used to be a good man. At least I thought he did. I guess I was just wrong." Synthia said as she looked down again, solemnly. "He decided that his career was more important than our family. I can rationalize him leaving me, but how he could leave his little boys? I just don't know how a person could do that." Synthia began crying.

Malcolm just sat still, trying to find words that didn't seem to come. He considered moving closer and putting a hand on her knee as a consoling gesture, but he refrained.

"I'm sorry to hear that, Miss Dobson." Malcolm's comment was followed by an awkward silence. "What does he do for a living?"

"He works for the water treatment facilities as a chemist. He works with the additives that go into the system." That response hit Malcolm like a ton of bricks. Synthia must have seen it on his face.

"What's wrong?"

"Oh, nothing. I'm sorry," Malcolm said as he shook his head to refocus. "What's his name?"

"Bruce Dobson." Right then a younger 6-year-old boy came into the front room.

"Are you okay, Mamma?"

Synthia smiled at him. "Yes, I'm fine sweetheart. Rex, this is Malcolm."

"Hi Rex." Malcolm put his hand out to shake. The little boy shook his hand and sat back by his mother.

"Thank you for taking time, Miss Dobson. I better get back on the road. I've got to get back to Colorado for school."

"Thank you for stopping by Malcolm." Synthia moved closer and put her hands on the hand Malcolm had resting on his knee. She looked him in the eyes and said sincerely, "It really means a lot to me."

Chapter 16

After meeting back in Colorado, Stephanie and Malcolm sat down at a coffee shop. At the counter, Malcolm ordered a coffee for both Stephanie and himself.

"You're drinking coffee?" Stephanie asked.

"Today I am. If we're going to be Project Caffeine, I figured I ought to at least try it," Malcolm said smiling.

"You're totally going to hell," Stephanie said in jest, and they both laughed.

"At least I'll be in good company." They raised their coffee mugs and clinked them together.

When meeting others at coffee shops, Malcolm usually ordered a steamed milk, with a couple squirts of vanilla. Besides a half a cup at Professor Temkin's house, Malcolm hadn't had a drink of coffee or alcohol since just before he left for college, which he chalked off as his rebellious teenage years. Coffee was forbidden in his religion. Other caffeinated drinks were acceptable, but hot caffeine could prevent one from entering the

Temple of God. That had never made sense to Malcolm, and it bothered him ever since he became old enough to conceptualize the contradiction. He had eventually resigned himself to the concept that we don't know all the reasons for what God does. Drinking a lot of caffeine probably isn't good, whether hot or cold, and not drinking coffee wasn't that big of a deal to Malcolm, so he just pushed it to the back recesses of his mind.

The truth was, Malcolm's belief system had been slowly changing over the last year. He saw contradictions and double talk more and more in the world around him. Although he somewhat held on to the religion of his youth and of his family, there was more and more that made him feel differently about God, religion, and life in general. This was his first real outward act of opposition to his faith in years, besides attending Sunday service a little less frequently.

"How did you never get caught up in the faith, being from Central Utah?" Malcolm asked Stephanie. Stephanie thought back in time for a moment.

"When I was young and many of my friends were getting baptized in the Mormon church, I asked my dad if I should get baptized too. He told me that the ultimate decision would be mine when I got a little older. 'But, what do you think?' I asked him again. He said, 'any faith that requires my little girl to have to depend on a man to receive all the blessings in this world and in heaven is just something that I don't believe. The Mormon church believes that the Priesthood, or power of God on earth, is only given to men. Steph,' he said, 'you don't need anyone else to obtain all that God is or has. It's within you. It's a part of you.' What he said to me that day always stuck with me." Malcolm thought about what she said and nodded. It made sense to him.

With coffee in hand, Malcolm and Stephanie began sharing with each other what they had discovered that pertained to their project. After sharing everything that they felt was relevant, they decided that the best lead for immediate follow-up was Richard Norton. They would attend school through Tuesday, then leave early Wednesday morning towards The Center for Disease Control in Atlanta.

After getting the cup of coffee down, Malcolm got up to use the restroom. He wasn't used to this level of caffeine and it ran through his system. When he returned, Stephanie was looking at her phone, scrolling through her Twitter account.

"Holy shit!"

"What's wrong?" asked Malcolm. Stephanie just continued to stare at her phone.

"What?"

"Our Embassy has just been raided and our Saudi Ambassador is dead."

"What?"

"It says they requested help and were denied assistance when the terrorists attacked and eventually overran the Embassy. It lasted 7 hours before the ambassador and several Marines were killed. What's worse, is that help was only 45 minutes away.

Malcolm pulled out his phone and searched the topic. Several of the news stations, briefly mentioned it before moving onto the weather, sports, and celebrity gossip. The only in-depth coverage was from the Central News System where it dominated their page.

"This supports exactly what we found earlier," Stephanie said. "This is big news. This is all that should be on the news, but the only one focusing on it is CNS!"

"Yeah, things are getting bad. Unless it impacts people directly, it doesn't seem to matter," Malcolm said. "And, I have a feeling it's going to get a lot worse before it gets better."

They sat silent for a moment, then Malcolm said,

"Tell me more about your trip back home. Could you see this linked into more than mosquito spray and the flu shot?"

"Polly, who works in the city building back home said that the federal government is regulating every chemical that comes into contact with people…insecticides, fluoride, you name it." Malcolm's eyes went wide,

"Fluoride?"

"Yeah, why?"

"I met a lady this weekend whose ex-husband is a chemist for a water treatment facility in California."

"Did he mention anything?"

"I didn't get to talk with him. He's the ex-husband. It's probably nothing. He's the local guy. Your friend said it's driven by the Federal Government, right? "

"Yeah, she did."

"It's an interesting coincidence though."

When Wednesday morning came, they spent the next 22 hours alternating between sleeping and driving. Late that night they arrived at their motel which was located just 10 minutes from the CDC. Before leaving, Stephanie had been able to talk to the Center for Disease Control, where Richard Norton worked. Stephanie had said that she and Malcolm were working on a school project focused on researching the impact of Health Services for the benefit of society. They had told her that she and Malcolm were welcome to schedule a brief meeting with Mr. Norton, but that they couldn't guarantee that Richard would be able to meet with them for more than just a couple of minutes.

At 7:00 AM, Stephanie and Malcolm arrived at the Volunteer Building where the CDC has an office on the sixth floor. After on-site security screening and after signing in, they were escorted up. When they arrived on the sixth floor, they met the Administrative Assistant, Darlene.

"Hello. How are you two doing?" she asked.

"We're well," answered Stephanie. "I believe I spoke to you on the phone," Stephanie continued, "I'm Stephanie Petersen and this is Malcolm Wright."

"Yes, I remember. A school project, right?"

"That's right. Does it look like Mr. Norton will have time to meet with us today?"

"Actually, you're in luck. He just had a meeting cancel."

Malcolm and Stephanie gave a quick glance towards one another, mixed with both relief and excitement.

"Let me see if he's ready for you."

After Darlene checked with him by phone, Mr. Norton came to the reception area. Richard Norton looked to be around 50, average height at about 5'10", short dark brown hair, with a touch of grey on the sides and an athletic build. When he came in, both Malcolm and Stephanie stood.

"Hello Mr. Norton, it's a pleasure to meet with you," Stephanie said, while extending her hand. "Thank you for taking time to speak with us." Richard shook hands with Stephanie.

"And, I'm Malcolm."

Mr. Norton shook his hand and said, "The pleasure is all mine. Let's come back to my office."

"So you are here on a school project?"

"Yes, we are, which makes us even more thankful for the time you're taking," answered Malcolm, "This impacts our grades." They all smiled.

"You've traveled quite a ways to meet with me. What would you like to know?"

Stephanie started in with questions, "What is the mission of the Department of Health Services?"

"To keep people healthy. We are constantly looking at the impact of disease and utilizing modern science to reduce or eliminate the negative impact that it has on society," Mr. Norton said.

Stephanie continued, "I read that in addition to self-inflicted diseases, like cardiovascular disease and diabetes, you are also very heavily involved in flu vaccines, fluoride in the water, and you work hand-in-hand with the Agriculture Department on agricultural herbicides. Is that right?"

"Well it looks like you have done your homework. I doubt you even need me," Mr. Norton said, again smiling.

"How involved are you at the implementation level? Are local state and city governments in charge of implementing these resources at the local level?"

"They absolutely are able to implement at a local level. We provide the research and data that moves towards elimination of these problems and the local governments initiate the tactical application."

"Mr. Norton, I have heard that local contractors are not allowed to purchase their own herbicides, flu vaccines, pesticides, or even fluoride for the water and that all of those things are provided exclusively by the federal government. Is that true?"

"Who told you that young lady?"

"I just wanted to be prepared before meeting with you to make this as productive as possible, so I spoke with local city governments around where we live."

Mr. Norton seemed to be a little irritated but answered, "In order to ensure that these products are produced correctly, we enforce strict standards during our production and then distribute the product to local municipalities. So, you are correct."

"Is it true that private companies develop the compounds, but then ship it to you for redistribution and that the true reproduction of these compounds are not actually produced by the federal government?"

Now even more annoyed, "Where are you going with this?"

"Well, it seems quite inefficient to manufacture this product in Texas, ship it to Atlanta and then ship it back to the West Coast. Have you ever had to send a batch back that did not meet federal specifications? And, why are private companies providing blood pressure and diabetes medications, but then you're having manufacturers send the flu vaccine back here?" Mr. Norton looked at his phone.

"Oh, it looks like they have decided to go ahead with my meeting after all. I apologize, but I'm going to have to run. I hope that this was helpful. Please come back some other time."

"Mr. Norton," Malcolm said, "we've just driven hundreds of miles to meet with you. Is there a time later today that we can come back?"

"Go ahead and check with Darlene up front. She knows my schedule better than I do. I apologize. Let me know if I can do anything else for you." Mr. Norton then stood up and escorted both Stephanie and Malcolm out through his office door. He closed his door after them and both Stephanie and Malcolm walked to the front reception area.

"Hi Darlene, it looks like Mr. Norton does have to go to his meeting. What time today can we come back to finish speaking with him?" asked Malcolm.

"Oh really? Well, let me see what we can do. We should be able to find something." While she was looking in her computer, her cell phone beeped. After looking at it, her demeanor changed.

"I'm sorry, it looks like Mr. Norton's schedule is packed full for the rest of the day."

"What about tomorrow? Can we meet him tomorrow?" Malcolm asked.

Darlene didn't even look at her computer this time. "I'm sorry, he's booked tomorrow too."

"When is the next time we can meet with him, Darlene," asked Stephanie urgently.

"I'm sorry, but it looks like it will be awhile."

"Did he tell you he didn't want to meet with us? Is that what the text said?"

"Miss, I'm sorry, but I am going to have to ask you to leave now. Thank you for coming by. I hope that you get all of the information that you need for your project."

Malcolm and Stephanie left the building and began walking to their car. Stephanie said, "There is definitely something that he does not want us to know."

"You think?" Malcolm said sarcastically. "Way to go pushing her on that text message. I would say our chance on getting back in there is nil."

"It was already nil. I just wanted her to know that we knew

what they were doing."

"What now?"

"Now we find out what's really going on."

"Ok. How?" A huge grin appeared on Stephanie's face.

"What?" asked Malcolm. Stephanie held up a small piece of paper with what looked to be an address on it.

"What's that?"

"This is our ticket in Malcolm." That small piece of paper held the address of a party that was taking place that night. Stephanie had flirtatiously leveraged her assets when Malcolm had gone to the restroom before going up to the sixth floor.

"This is at the security guard's house. If we can get ahold of his access card, we can get back in there and see what he's hiding in those file cabinets."

Chapter 17

"How did you know where to get that?" asked Stephanie when Malcolm came back to their hotel room with Rohypnol, the notorious "date-rape" drug.

"This brother has connections…fortunately not all of them are on the up and up."

"I hope to God, you've never used something like that!"

"I never would. It's disgusting and despicable, but before I decided on my Sociology Major, I had considered Criminal Justice. I took a chance and asked some characters loitering on the street if I could score some. Within 15 minutes, I had this."

"Wow, it's unbelievable how easy that is to get."

"Unbelievable and scary," Malcolm responded, "Don't ever let someone you don't know well, get your drink for you."

"No, I don't think I will."

"Now Steph, it's up to you to get it in the security guard's drink."

They arrived at John Garland's house at 8:00 PM that night. Both Malcolm and Stephanie were dressed ready to party. Stephanie had taken particular time to wear something classy, but definitely sexy. She wore a tight, blue sleeveless dress that fit in such a way to further gain the attention of their host. Before going in, Malcolm had instructed Stephanie to get it in his drink and to wait until she saw signs of him getting groggy before helping him to his room.

"You want to wait until you start seeing the effects of the drug, probably around 30 minutes, or taking one for the team may mean a little more than you originally intended. But, pay attention, because once it starts to work, the effects come on fast. Once you're ready to take him to his room, if you don't see me in the same area that you're in, text me and I'll follow within the next couple of minutes."

They walked up to the door and John answered their knock.

"You came! I wasn't sure you would make it."

"I told you I would do all I could to make it here," answered Stephanie.

"Is this your boyfriend?"

"She wishes," Malcolm said with a smile, extending his hand. "I'm Malcolm. We're just working on a project for school together."

"Good to meet you Malcolm."

Malcolm could see the relief in his eyes as John realized they weren't dating. *This is a good sign*, Malcolm thought to himself. Stephanie played her part well--flirtatious, but not desperate. Just the right balance of *I'm interested, but you're going to have to work at it to make it happen.*

Malcolm separated from the two and began mingling with the others at the party. After small talk with several small groups of people and some bantering back and forth about football teams, Malcolm took a seat in the living room to locate where Stephanie and John had ended up. The layout of the house was quite open. From the front door, you walked into the living room. To the right was a dining room with a long table packed with appetizers. Straight ahead was the kitchen with a bar separating the living room from the kitchen. Beyond the kitchen was a sliding glass door that led to a wooden balcony. Malcolm could see Stephanie smiling and engaged in cheerful discussion with John, another woman, and another man that Malcolm thought he recognized as another security guard at the CDC.

"Hey there." Malcolm was taken by surprise. He hadn't even noticed this hard bodied, petite Latina woman approach.

"Hi."

"I don't think we've met, I'm Alicia."

"I'm Malcolm. Pleased to meet you."

"Are you friends with John?"

"Oh, um, no. We met today. He invited a friend of mine that I'm traveling with from Denver."

"Denver? What brought you here from Denver?"

"Just a project for school around disease eradication and

the impact on society. Not exactly a party conversation," Malcolm said smiling.

"Well, I think that's hot," Alicia said as she smiled back and took a seat up against him on the sofa. She put her hand on his thigh and said, "Tell me about it."

Malcolm wanted to do a lot more than tell her about it, and from what he could tell, so did she. They engaged in flirtatious small talk for a couple of minutes before Malcolm remembered what he was doing. When he looked up to where Stephanie had been, she was gone. The two others who had been speaking to John and Stephanie were still there.

Oh shit, Malcolm thought. "Excuse me just for a minute. I've got to use the restroom," Malcolm told Alicia.

"Do you need help in there?"

"I'll be right back," he replied with a smile.

He took a small tour around the house to make sure that they hadn't gotten up to get a drink, and then he looked outside on the patio. He didn't see them anywhere. Malcolm walked up the stairs to where he assumed the bedrooms were. There were three closed doors at the top of the staircase. One right at the top of the stairs, one to his right and one to his left. He opened the door right in front of him and found the laundry room. He went down the short hall to his left and opened the door there.

"This room's taken!" yelled out an unfamiliar man on top of his date for the night.

"Sorry," said Malcolm and he shut the door. Malcolm went

to his right and tried the third door. It was locked. He felt a panic grow inside of him. *What if things were not going as planned?* He went back to the middle door and went into the laundry room. Inside were a couple of wire hangers. He grabbed one and straightened the end to use as a key. He put it into the small hole in the doorknob of the locked room and turned the handle. It opened. He opened it slowly and looked in. It was definitely the master bedroom, but it didn't look like anyone was inside. He continued in. Malcolm flipped on the light and looked quickly around the room for the security guard's badge.

Outside Stephanie and John were talking when John noticed his bedroom light turn on.

"What the fuck man! Get out of my room!" he yelled from outside. He turned from Stephanie and started walking back into the house.

"I'm sure it's nothing." Stephanie said.

"I locked that door. Nobody should be in there!" He continued in. Stephanie had slipped the drug in his drink about 15 minutes earlier. John left the cup, still halfway full, where they had been talking outside.

Inside Malcolm rifled through his drawers, trying to find the badge. Less than a minute later John burst into the room.

"What the fuck are you doing?" John exclaimed. The words came out, but the latter half of his sentence trailed off and he stretched a hand out towards his dresser to steady himself. *The drugs*, Malcolm thought.

"Are you okay buddy? Come sit down." Stephanie now entered the room.

"What are you doing with my shit?" John said.

"I just chased some asshole out of your room and wanted to make sure everything was okay," Malcolm replied. He looked up at Stephanie, telling her with his eyes what he was trying to do. She answered back with a slight nod and Malcolm knew that the drugs were working on John.

"I just saw some guy run out the front," Stephanie said. "Thank you for stopping him Malcolm."

"Yeah, thanks man," John said. "I don't feel right." John was sitting on the bed. "Come on. Lay back. It will make you feel better," Malcolm said. John laid back. A few minutes later, he was out.

A couple of John's larger security guard friends showed up outside John's bedroom door. One was around 6'2" with dark brown hair and a muscular linebacker build. The other was blonde, about the same height--still muscular, but more like a triathlete than a football player.

"Everything okay in there?"

"Yeah, I think he just had a little too much to drink. He's lying down for a minute," Stephanie said.

Malcolm and Stephanie then walked briskly down the steps and towards the front door of the house. When they reached the front door, one of John's friends yelled, "Hey, stop them!" A man near the front door slammed the door shut as Malcolm had just begun to open it. The man then stepped in-between Malcolm and the door, while others at the party began to surround them.

"What the fuck did you do to him?" the dark haired stocky friend yelled, now just standing a couple of feet from Malcolm. Malcolm didn't say anything; he just backed up. The man at the door pushed him from behind and he fell forward into the stocky man. He grabbed Malcolm by the shirt, pulling his face towards his and said again,

"What the fuck did you do to John?"

"He didn't do anything. Let him go," pleaded Stephanie. She stood just a few feet away.

"Does anybody know these people?" the stocky man yelled. The entire party was now gathered around Malcolm and Stephanie.

"John invited us!" Stephanie exclaimed. "Let him go!" The stocky man threw Malcolm to the ground.

"Why do you care about this nigger?" the stocky man growled at Stephanie as he took a step towards her. He looked her up and down.

"You ever get fucked by a real man, you dirty bitch?" He grabbed her tightly on her sides with both hands.

"Please, just let us go," pleaded Stephanie. Malcolm tried to get up, but was thrown back down by the blond slender man.

"It's up to you," said the stocky man to Stephanie. "You come play with me for a little while, or we lynch this fucking nigger." With tears in her eyes, Stephanie looked down at

Malcolm and then back at the man standing before her.

"I'll come with you, just leave him alone," sobbed Stephanie. The blond slender man was still standing over Malcolm, but his head was turned towards Stephanie. Malcolm kicked him in the groin as hard as he could. As the man pitched over, Malcolm sprung to his feet, grabbed the back of the blond man's head with both hands and thrust his knee into his face with all the force he had. The man dropped and blood sprayed out from his nose. Malcolm turned everything he had towards the stocky man, hitting him in the face with a right cross. The man stumbled back. Malcolm felt a hard blow to the left side of his head, then another blow came from the other side. As he covered up, fists from all directions pummeled him. He was knocked to the ground and the punches turned into a flurry of kicks from all directions. The next thing Malcolm heard was the sound of sirens followed by the flash of red and blue lights, then. . . everything went dark.

Chapter 18

Malcolm opened his eyes and saw his mother sitting on the edge of his hospital bed. "I'm here honey. I'm here." He looked into her face. Inside the tired lines of being overworked and overstretched to provide for her and her children, love and concern poured out.

"I'm sorry, Malcolm. I should have been there honey." He looked down at his six-year-old body where he saw the bruises left from being held down and felt the pain inside from being penetrated. His tears began to flow. "I'm sorry Momma. I'm sorry Momma."

Tears flowed even heavier and his body shook as he sobbed.

"Malcolm," he heard his mother's voice say.

"Malcolm." The voice became more distant and dreamlike.

"Malcolm." It was almost hollow now.

"Malcolm." It began to become more clear, as the words sounded closer. It was no longer his mother, it was Stephanie.

"Malcolm," he heard again as he struggled to open his eyes. He blinked trying to adjust to the light.

"It's okay Malcolm," said Stephanie, as she leaned over him in his hospital room.

The reality of that evening began to set in. He remembered the party and what had happened. Real tears started to flow down his cheeks.

"I tried to stop them. I tried."

"You did Malcolm. You did," Stephanie said with a small grateful smile. "Thank you. Thank you so much."

Later Malcolm would contemplate that dream on many occasions. His mother never knew what abuse had happened until that night he told his parents during his ninth year of life. He could sense the guilt that his mother had felt around allowing something like this to happen to her son. He knew that she wished she had been there for him at that moment. That haunted him and was even more painful to Malcolm than his own wounds. He blamed himself for causing his mother to feel like that.

Chapter 19

Professor Walker walked into Malcolm's hospital room the day after he was admitted.

"Hello Malcolm. How are you holding up?"

"Professor. What are you doing here?"

"Stephanie called and shared with me some of the things you're finding." The professor moved closer to Malcolm and sat on the edge of his bed.

"It sounds like this could run very deep and that some powerful people could be behind some of what's going on. I'm sorry for getting you and Stephanie involved in this. I've also had some people around campus asking about what you're working on."

"What? Who?" asked Malcolm.

"The Dean called me yesterday, asking specifically what you two were working on. A man from the federal government working for the CIA mentioned that you two had been inquiring about widespread disease and vaccines utilized broadly within the

United States. He was following up on a concern regarding biologic terrorism and wanted specific details on the assignment. I was asked to pull you two off of this project and to align your work with the rest of the class."

"Professor, we can't stop now. This is too big."

"I know Malcolm, but you need to be aware of what you're getting into. Be careful. Don't trust anyone within the government. I'm not sure how far this goes up, and we need to be aligned in what we say is going on."

That afternoon, Professor Walker flew back to Colorado, and Malcolm was released from the hospital. As they exited the main entrance of the hospital, two men in suits stopped Malcolm and Stephanie. One was African American with a medium build, standing about 5'10". The other was Caucasian, with a similar build.

"Malcolm Wright and Stephanie Petersen?" asked the African American.

"Yes?" answered Stephanie.

"I'm Special Agent Jeremiah Watson. This is my partner, Special Agent Truman Sikes. We would like to have a word with you."

"What's going on?" asked Malcolm.

"Come with us." Malcolm caught a brief glimpse of a gun on the right hip of Agent Watson as he turned to lead them to their vehicle. A badge was on his left hip.

"Are we in trouble for something?" asked Stephanie.

"We just want to ask you some questions. It won't take long," answered Agent Sikes.

Stephanie and Malcolm followed them to their black sedan. Agent Sikes opened the rear door for them, and they both got in. Both of the agents got in the car, with Agent Watson in the driver's seat.

"Where are you taking us?" asked Malcolm. Neither one of the men answered.

About 10 minutes later, they arrived at a plain three-story beige building, with a gate and a guard outside. As they pulled into the entrance, a guard stepped out of a small station. Agent Watson showed him an ID and they continued in. Within the next 15 minutes, they were sitting in a third floor meeting room with a table separating them from Agent Sikes. Agent Watson was still standing.

"Can I get you two something to drink?" he asked.

"No thank you," answered Malcolm. Stephanie just shook her head.

Special Agent Watson took a seat across from them and just looked at them for a moment.

"So, I hear that you are working on a school project. Is that right?" he asked.

"Yes," answered Stephanie.

"It's on the impact of disease reduction and eradication on society?" he asked, while reading from a notepad he held. "And how does that relate to a Sociology project?" asked Agent Sikes.

"That seems more in line with a course in health."

Stephanie continued the story that she and Malcolm had discussed with Professor Walker,

"The impact of disease, and even more importantly, the perceived impact of disease, can have a significant impact on both individual psychology, as well as societal behavior. Our goal is to determine the extent of that impact, as well as clearly define the specific items that impact society as a whole and how this impacts group behavior."

"What have you done to research this project to date?" asked Agent Watson.

Malcolm answered, "We have pretty much just done research on the web and then took a trip down here to meet with the CDC to further that research." He deliberately left out his visit with Professor Temkin in California and the link that Stephanie had uncovered with Mr. Norton in Marysvale.

"What were you two doing at John Garland's house?" asked Agent Watson.

"He invited me to a party," replied Stephanie.

"What happened at that party," asked Agent Sikes.

"Well, it seems that they don't take kindly to colored folks, especially when they show up with a white woman," Malcolm answered.

They all sat silent for a moment. Agent Watson then started, "Biologic terrorism is a threat we take very seriously. Activities that you two have been involved in are consistent with attempts that have been made to cause harm to large groups of people."

"We're not terrorists," exclaimed Malcolm.

"What has your involvement with Islam been?" asked Agent Sikes.

"Islam? I'm Christian sir."

"Using Christian cover has recently been utilized to cover radical Muslim ties to terrorist organizations originating within Afghanistan. You are both being watched closely."

Agent Watson then leaned towards both Malcolm and Stephanie, looking into Malcolm's eyes, and then Stephanie's. "Be careful with what you get involved in."

The meaning of those words seemed to have meaning beyond the terrorist allegations. His eyes and demeanor saying, *I know what you are looking into. If you pursue this further, there will be trouble.*

A few hours later, after being dropped off at the hospital to retrieve their car, both Stephanie and Malcolm were on their way back to Colorado. Eight and a half hours into the drive, they arrived in St. Louis, Missouri. They pulled into a Super 8 motel. When they went to check-in, the attendant only had a queen size bed available.

"Are there any two double bed options?" Malcolm asked.

"I'm sorry sir, that's all we have available." Malcolm looked at Stephanie.

"It's fine," she said.

She took his arm and placed her head on his shoulder for a moment. Malcolm gave the hotel attendant his credit card to take care of the charges and they both walked across the parking lot to their room.

"I can sleep on the floor, Steph. It's no big deal," Malcolm said.

"No, after all that's happened I want to be close to you. Is that okay?"

Malcolm nodded his head, smiled, and said, "of course."

That evening they connected at a deeper level, both emotionally and physically. After making love, Stephanie laid her head on his chest. He played with her hair until she fell asleep. Malcolm laid there running through all that had happened since both he and Stephanie had started on the project.

Malcolm also reflected back to well before this project had started, even before he had met Stephanie and before he even began attending Denver University. As a child, Malcolm had felt guilt and betrayal for the abuse he had endured as a young child. He used to talk to God, asking, "Why? Why has this happened to me?" He remembered wishing that there was no such thing as sex. It was sex that he encountered in the form of sexual abuse that tainted the world around him. This concept evolved for Malcolm as he moved into his teenage years. He could feel the pain of others that had encountered similar experiences. He reflected on his journal entry that said, "It's as if I was sent here to help others." His own pain acted as a portal to get inside and understand the turmoil of others, who were often engulfed in a deeper sense of hell, and to help them navigate to a place that was more tolerable…a place where peace, even if just for a moment, resided.

But, with that presence for others, he still dealt with his own demons. He strived to make what was "bad," good. He went from avoiding the thoughts of sex to engulfing himself in it. As a teenage boy and young man, his conquests of sleeping with girls was widely accepted. The girls who did the same thing were looked down upon and even shamed for acts they had committed with multiple people. On many occasions, while in bed, he saw that injustice and knew why they did what they did, yet he fed into it anyway. He had the opportunity to help them see more of themselves, beyond just a method of pleasure for another. But, he did indulge himself, oftentimes then leaving the girl and the situation in order to escape himself.

Embracing religion had helped him step outside of the false reality and the self-destructive acts that he was involved in. They did not stop at promiscuous activity, but also were full of mind-numbing drugs and alcohol. As he found himself deeper in religion years later, he also saw a part that fed into a similar dysfunction. It just took another form, a form hidden within rituals and covenants that the followers promise to obey. A feeling of guilt followed the saints, like the guilt that Malcolm had felt from his abuse. It was a guilt of being unclean and not good enough…never good enough. Many of the church followers were actors. Professing one thing on Sunday and acting another way on

Monday. Malcolm's own abuser was very active in the church, and even held church priesthood positions.

Thoughts and anxious feelings grew within Malcolm as he wondered if there is truth…if there is a God. Everywhere that he seemed to turn to find solace, stood the wolf in sheep's clothing. At every turn, just as he felt a brief reprieve from the world, he encountered a façade that appeared to be pointing towards God, but revealed the sharp teeth beneath the wool. Tears ran down Malcolm's cheeks. He did what he could to control the sobs, as to not wake Stephanie. "God, if there is a God, please help me. I don't know what to do."

A warmth and calming filled him. "Be still, and know that I am God," Psalm 46:10, echoed through his mind. The peace continued to sweep over him. A feeling of, *there's more to life than you know and there is more to you than what you've come to know as Malcolm*, resonated within him. His tears had stopped and his breathing had slowed. Again, his mind wandered back to his childhood journal entry. It's as if he was sent here to help others. With Stephanie still asleep in his arms, with her head upon his chest, he touched her face and then fell asleep.

Chapter 20

Around 6:00 AM the following morning, Malcolm woke to the early light coming through the slit in the motel curtains and to the sound and smell of the motel coffee machine starting to brew. As he looked around the room, he could see Stephanie's figure pouring another cup of water into the top of the coffee maker. He could see the smooth lines of her body, wearing only a tight tank top and a pair of his boxer shorts. She seemed to almost glide as she went through the motions. Malcolm had not seen her this way before or at least hadn't allowed himself to indulge on the feelings he felt move through him for this woman. She looked back over at him.

"Hey there sleepy head," she said with a smile.

She walked over to the bed. Malcolm put his arm out to clear a spot for her to join him. She lay beside him with her head on his chest and her arm around his waist.

"How are you doing?" Stephanie asked.

"I'm good. How are you?"

"Really good," she replied as she squeezed him tightly.

Forty-five minutes later they were on the road and stopped at a Flying J, just off of the highway, to grab some more coffee and a couple of snacks for the trip.

"Welcome to Flying J," the male clerk at the counter said in a feminine voice.

Malcolm looked over at the clerk. He was quite flamboyant in the way he spoke and grabbed the items a customer had brought to the counter.

"What brings you around here?" the clerk asked Malcolm, while smiling and cocking his head to the side.

"Just passing through," Malcolm answered.

The scene brought Malcolm back to his junior year in high school. He and a group of 5 other guys had gone down to a park near the old downtown center of Colorado Springs to drink some beer away from anywhere their parents or friends of their parents would see them. Across the street from the southeast corner of the park, near some old run-down buildings, was a gay bar called the Blue Oyster. Malcolm had heard stories of others cruising past the place to "gay bash," which was basically jumping out to beat up a lone gay man walking out of the bar. After several boys beat on the man, they would jump back in the car with the lights out to avoid getting the plate reported. Malcolm had never participated before, but as they sat there drinking, several of the boys he was with started making plans to do it.

Malcolm had a brother named Ray who had been gay. He

was 5 years older than Malcolm. Though having feminine tendencies, he wasn't obviously flamboyant. After a high school stomp, which was what they had called their casual school dances, a group of 5 football players from the school, with several of the cheerleaders, walked out of the gym into the parking lot. Before they got into their cars, they saw Ray's car parked across the school parking lot in front of the LDS Church Seminary building. Given Ray's feminine qualities and awkwardness around some of the guys, he was often a target of bullying.

"Hey, what's Ray-tard doing at the church," one of the boys asked the rest of the group.

"Let's go invite him to play," another commented. "You'd do him right Maddie?"

Maddie flipped the boy off and the other guys laughed. They continued to walk over towards Ray's car. They could see a faint image of someone moving inside.

"He's in there. Be quiet." Moving closer to his car, they crouched down to avoid being seen. When they got to the car, they saw Ray and another person making out. One of the boys yelled,

"Ray-tards a fucking fagot!" Another one of the football players flung open the door.

"Get out of the car fagot! God doesn't like fagots and your grabbing dick at his house!"

They tore Ray and the other boy out of the car and threw a flurry of punches and kicks at them. Halfway through the beating, the boy that Ray was with managed to get up and run away. At the end of the beating Ray was knocked out with a broken and bleeding face. He also suffered 4 broken ribs and a punctured lung. Over the next three weeks, Ray spent time at McKay-Dee Hospital recovering. Malcolm's parents were engulfed within an emotional frenzy. Not only had one of their sons been beaten nearly to death but, in their minds, something worse had occurred. They had discovered their son was gay. This proved to be too much for Malcolm's parents. They soon separated, which was then followed by an inevitable divorce.

Malcolm paid for their coffee and snacks and got into the car with Stephanie. With two steaming cups of coffee in the car's cup holder, they were on their way to Denver. Fifteen minutes into their drive, Stephanie asked,

"Are you okay Malcolm?"

"Yeah, I'm alright, just thinking."

"About what?" she asked.

"Did I ever tell you that I had an older brother?"

"What do you mean you HAD an older brother?"

"He killed himself in high school, while I was just finishing my last year of grade school."

"Oh, I'm so sorry. What happened?"

"He was gay."

"Oh," Stephanie said in a way that made Malcolm feel like she understood why he killed himself. Malcolm got the feeling that her response came from a place where gay was not a good option and that death may have been a reasonable alternative.

Malcolm let the conversation rest and they drove on. But his mind continued to think about that night near the Blue Oyster. While the others jeered each other on and pumped each other up waiting for their victim, Malcolm sat in the back seat, full of anxiety and dread. It had been five and a half years since his brother's death. None of these boys knew about his gay brother, and he preferred to keep it that way. With hundreds of miles between Colorado Springs and Ogden, they were not likely to ever find out, unless Malcolm told them. As the boys waited, several groups of three to four men walked out of the bar, but multiple men were too dangerous for the teenagers to consider starting trouble with. They were waiting for a lone man to exit.

A police car rolled up and parked outside of the bar. Malcolm and the others tried to hide their beers near their feet in the backseat. Two officers exited their car and went into the bar. As soon as the officers were out of sight, afraid of being caught with alcohol, the driver of the car started it and drove away. Malcolm had felt relief as they drove away, but still an awful and sick feeling resided in his gut about what had almost occurred. As he drove towards Denver, he asked himself if he really could have participated that day, years ago. There was no way he would ever find himself considering it now, but still, he couldn't say what would have happened back then if the police car had not shown up and if a lone gay man had walked out of the bar.

During their drive, Malcolm had tuned their radio onto the National Public Radio station. A couple of hours into the ride, they heard a familiar voice.

"We want to urge all Americans to get their flu vaccines. The CDC has been working with pharmaceutical companies to increase production of the vaccine to ensure all citizens are protected from the lethal alteration of the H1N1 strain that has made it to the United States from Africa." The voice was that of Richard Norton.

"This is getting out of control," Stephanie said, looking over at Malcolm.

"It's been out of control. We're just starting to see it."

"What are we going to do?"

"All we can do," Malcolm answered. "I'm going to give Professor Temkin a call. He's got to know more that can help us." Malcolm dialed the professor's number. After several rings, he picked up.

"Hello."

"Hello, Professor. This is Malcolm. Can you talk?"

"I don't know any Malcolm and I don't have time for any more sales calls!"

The phone went dead. Malcolm redialed his number. It rang once then went to voicemail. Malcolm waited a minute then called again. Again it went to voicemail.

"Damn it! Why won't he talk to me!" Stephanie put her hand on his arm.

"They must have gotten to him," Stephanie answered as tears welled up in her eyes. "They're going to get us Malcolm. We can't keep doing this. They're going to get us too."

"They can't do anything to us Steph. We haven't done anything. Let's just calm down. We'll figure it out." Several minutes later Malcolm's phone rang. The number on the caller ID wasn't familiar.

"Hello." It was Professor Temkin.

"Hi Malcolm. I'm sorry about what just happened. We are dealing with very powerful people. Their access to phone records and all types of information is beyond what you would comprehend. Pick up a prepaid phone and call me at this number."

"We need your help," Malcolm urged.

"We can't talk now. Do what I say and we'll go from there." The line then went dead as Professor Temkin hung up his phone.

"Was that Professor Temkin?" Stephanie asked.

Malcolm nodded his head. "What did he say? Will he help us?"

Malcolm filled her in on the specifics. An hour later they pulled into a Wal-Mart and picked up a prepaid phone.

When they got to the car, Stephanie went to the driver's side. "I'll drive for a while so you can call the professor back."

After they got in, Malcolm powered on the prepaid phone and dialed up the professor. He answered after a couple of rings.

"Hello"

"Hello Professor?"

"Hi Malcolm. It's good to hear from you. How are you

holding up?"

Malcolm told him about what they had experienced since he had seen the professor at his home in California.

"Yes, it goes up very high Malcolm. There are top leaders of this country involved, which very likely could include the President of the United States."

"It goes all the way to the president?"

"I've not confirmed his direct involvement. He is either naïve or distancing himself just enough to avoid trouble should any negative fallout come from what's going on."

Chapter 21

Hours later, Malcolm, who had switched places with Stephanie again, pulled up in front of her apartment. He got out and walked her to her door. They hugged and kissed.

"What do you think about last night?" Malcolm asked.

"I think that I've fallen for you and want you all to myself," answered Stephanie. "What do you think?"

"I think you can have me all to yourself. I've fallen for you too," Malcolm said. They both smiled, kissed and hugged again as they said their goodbyes.

After leaving Stephanie, Malcolm continued on to his own apartment. As he reached the bottom of the stairs, Reggie yelled out to him,

"Malcolm! Wait up brotha!" Reggie and Cliff jogged to catch up.

"Where you been man?" said Cliff as they clapped hands and embraced with a half hug. Reggie followed up the same way.

As they walked up the stairs, they filled Malcolm in on the

regular college happenings, like parties gone bad and partying going awry with some of the people they all knew. As they reached their floor on the third level, Malcolm stopped.

"Were you guys just here?" asked Malcolm.

"Nah man, you know we got practice," answered Reggie.

"You left the door open man," scolded Cliff as he gave a look to Reggie.

"I didn't leave it open. I know I locked it up. They're probably just fixin something you broke!" Reggie said back to Cliff.

Both Cliff and Reggie could see the worry on Malcolm's face.

"Why you trippin man. I'm sure it's nothin," said Reggie.

"I hope someone's breakin in" said Cliff. "I'll woop up on that motherfucker!" he continued as he walked faster towards their apartment door.

"Hold up," said Malcolm in a hushed, but urgent tone. "Crazy shits been happening man. Be careful."

They walked more slowly now as they approached the door.

"Someone's in there," warned Reggie.

Cliff took the lead through the door. The three desks in the living area had all the drawers pulled out and paper was thrown throughout the room. A rustling noise came from Malcolm's bedroom. Cliff, with his large and daunting frame walked straight in.

"What the fuck you doing?" Cliff exclaimed.

The two men in the room looked up in surprise, but quickly refocused on their next task at hand, namely Cliff. They looked like they could have been college age, but something about them seemed older, more experienced, even professional. One man sprayed Cliff in the eyes with what must have been some type of pepper spray. The other flung open a baton, like what police often wear on their belts, and struck Cliff on the side of the head with a crashing blow. Cliff dropped.

The two men came out of Malcolm's bedroom. Reggie engaged with the quickness others respected him for on the field and struck the man with the club in the face with a heavy right hand. The other man moved around Reggie's right side and struck him under the arm with a Taser. Reggie flinched from 8000 volts. Like a trained assassin, the man slipped behind Reggie, moved his hand and arm across Reggie's throat and caught him in a blood choke. Malcolm stepped forward and hit the man on the right side of his face. He didn't let go. He just buried his head in closer to Reggie's back to avoid another blow from Malcolm and swung Reggie around to be positioned between him and Malcolm. Reggie's body fell limp and the man let go as Reggie started dropping to the ground. Malcolm could see the attacker's laser-like focus turn towards him. Malcolm swung with his left, which the attacker slipped, and Malcolm followed with a quick right that just skimmed the top of the man's head. The attacker countered with an uppercut. Right at that moment, Malcolm heard a large bang and all went black.

Chapter 22

When Stephanie got to her room, two of her roommates were getting ready to go out.

"You're just in time!" Nicki exclaimed. "Get on your sexy stuff, we're going out."

"Thanks, but I'm not feeling up to it," Stephanie answered.

Marci chimed in, "Come on girl. You haven't hung out with us in forever. And, you look like you need it."

After several more minutes of persuading, Stephanie changed her clothes and headed out with the girls. Stephanie wasn't in the party mood, but the thought of being alone scared her.

Chapter 23

Malcolm woke up a few minutes later. He could smell spent gunpowder in the air. A surreal shock and fear struck him and culminated within his entire body. He imagined it as something similar to what those on the battlefield may experience as their reality takes a turn towards the unfathomable. He looked around the room and tried to gain his bearings. Reggie was sitting up, leaning against the wall near where he had fallen, just staring blankly forward.

"You alright bro?"

The voice came from behind him. He turned his head to see Cliff sitting on the couch. He was leaning over with his forearms resting on his massive thighs. There was a large gash on the side of his head. Blood had run down his face onto the right side of his chest and forearm. He looked out of it. Malcolm's gaze refocused onto the coffee table where a Glock 40 caliber handgun sat. He continued to scan the room. To his right, just a few feet from him lie the man who had knocked him out. His shirt was stained red and his body lie face down with his upper torso surrounded in a pool of crimson red. Cliff broke the silence,

"I shot him."

"Did you call the police?" asked Malcolm.

Cliff shook his head no. Malcolm had never seen Cliff like this. This massive man, with muscles that elicit envy from nearly everyone in his presence, almost seemed small and defeated.

"Why haven't you called the cops?"

Cliff just shook his head. "I shot him in the back, Malcolm." After he said it, there were several seconds of silence. Then, Cliff said it again. "I shot him in the back…"

It all began to register to Malcolm. He looked over at Reggie. He was looking down, just shaking his head. The magnitude of the situation sunk in even further. Trying to defend killing a man in self-defense after shooting him in the back was hard enough, but the fact that Cliff, a black man from the projects, having shot a white man in the back was even worse.

Cliff had thought that he had at last escaped his past. Football had provided a way out of the gangs that plagued those who grew up on the streets of Cleveland. He still bore tattoos as a constant reminder of who he was…the part of him he could never escape, and the part of him that now bore its face again in their college dorm. Cliff never knew his father. His mother did what she could, but hopelessness ran wild within the projects. His two older brothers had already been in and out of prison. His older sister was a junky, with kids from several men. Cliff was the rock, the hope, and football was the way.

Cliff himself had been arrested as a teen for shoplifting and loitering. During his freshmen year he had gone out for the football team and dominated the field. As his sophomore year started, he didn't even show up for tryouts. In the months before, he had been working all summer, saving money for clothes, cleats, and a coat for school, by stocking and moving boxes in and out of a warehouse for a paper supply company. Cliff stored the money he saved in a Nike shoe box under his bed. One evening after work in late August, he came home to find his oldest brother Rassan and Rassan's friends drinking and smoking weed in the living room. He walked past the boys to his room. The orange Nike box was on his bed, open and empty. Rage overtook Cliff as he walked out his bedroom door.

"Where the fuck is my money, Roc?"

Roc was Rassan's street name, which was a play on his name and what he was rumored to sell. His brother ignored him. The anger and adrenaline intensified even further. Cliff stormed towards Roc and threw him up against the wall. He grabbed his brother by the shirt, lifting him up so that his significantly shorter older brother and he were nose to nose and said,

"Where-the-fuck-is-my-money?"

"You're no better than me. When you gonna realize? You ain't nothing but nigga, just like me." Cliff let go, but his brother's words never left.

The next day, when he went back to work, he had an

incident. One of the other teens stocking boxes dropped his load of paper products near Cliff, landing on his foot.

"What the fuck are you doing?" Cliff yelled as he pushed the teen.

The boy was a couple years older than Cliff, but not bigger. He stepped up to Cliff, got out a "Fuck Y…" before Cliff knocked him out. Cliff was fired and spent the last few weeks of summer on the streets, following through with what his brother's words had taught him who he was.

On those streets is where his high school football coach, Parrish Rand, found him. Football conditioning had already started. Parrish came by 3 times trying to get Cliff to realize his talent and the opportunity football could provide for him.

"Football can save you Cliff…get you outta this neighborhood. I know what you're goin' through son. It will save your life. Don't you want more than this? Let me give you more, Son."

He had also asked Cliff to live with him during the school year. Cliff turned the coach down each time. That last time coach Rand asked, Cliff was not closer than he had been the first two times he'd been asked, but the night following that final offer, changed his perspective.

It was 9:00 PM and he was lying on his bed listening to music when he heard a hard knock on the door. When he unlatched the door it was forcefully pushed open by the Cleveland police on the other side of it. They came in with guns and vests, forcing Cliff to the ground. They handcuffed him and searched the house. A black cop put his knee in the middle of Cliff's back and said,

"Where the fuck is Roc?"

"Man, I don't know."

"Don't get smart with me."

The cop on top of him put his gun to back of Cliff's head.

"You're just a worthless street nigger. I could shoot you right now and the world wouldn't give a shit. You wanna die nigger?"

After a minute of silence, the cop got off of Cliff, kicked him in the side and they all left.

Cliff showed up to practice the next day. The following week he was living with coach Rand. During his remaining years of high school, although coming home often to help his mother, he spent more nights living with coach Rand during the school year than he did at home. Outside of fall football, there was winter weight training and spring strength and speed work that coach Rand used as reason for Cliff to stay with him beyond just the regular season.

Fifteen minutes after calling 911, the police and paramedics arrived. The police came in with hands on their guns, but kept them holstered, while directing Malcolm, Reggie, and Cliff to assume the position. They were all handcuffed while the police questioned them separately about what had happened there just an hour earlier. The police lead the boys out of the apartment and into the parking lot where the squad cars and ambulance were parked. The cuffs had been taken off of Reggie and Malcolm, but remained on Cliff. Reggie and Malcolm were put in one car. Cliff was placed alone in the second.

Chapter 24

Stephanie and her roommates walked into Kierstein, a local bar and dance club that was popular with the DU college students. It was loud and alive with energy. As they walked through, they could feel the throbbing base vibrate through them. The girls made their way over to the bar to get a drink, yelling hello over the music to others they knew in the club along the way.

"Tequila shooters all around," Marci ordered at the bar.

"Really?" Stephanie said to Marci as the bartender tended to their drinks.

"If anything's going to help you feel better, it's a tequila shooter!" she replied back.

After licking the salt, shooting the tequila, and sucking the lime, Marci and Nicki threw their hands up in the air yelling, "WOOOOOO." Stephanie smiled and rolled her eyes.

"Let's dance!" yelled Marci, and she started her way out towards the dance floor.

"Come on girl!" Nicki called to Stephanie. Stephanie

waved them off.

"Go ahead. I'll catch up in a minute." She had made it this far, but was far from being in a party mood. Stephanie ordered a Cosmo and sipped on it, trying to lighten the heavy feeling she now carried with her. Three quarters through her drink, a man took the stool next to Stephanie.

"Long Island Iced Tea and another drink for the lady," he said to the bar tender. He now turned towards her, "If that's okay with you?"

"Sure," Stephanie answered. She was already feeling the warm buzz flow through her body. It felt good. It felt like release.

"I don't know if we've ever formally met; I'm Mark."

"I'm Stephanie. Pleased to meet you."

"Oh, I know who you are. I've looked forward to meeting you for a while now."

"Oh you have, have you?"

"Definitely," Mark said smiling, and they lightly shook hands.

As the night went on they continued to make small talk, flirt, and drink together. Stephanie remembered seeing Mark around campus and at parties. He was fairly tall, around 6'1", with short brown hair, a muscular build and good looking.

Stephanie's phone rang from inside her small purse. She looked at the screen and saw that it was Malcolm. She denied the incoming call, turned the phone off, took Mark's hand and went out on the dance floor. On the floor, they danced close and seductively. They kissed and Mark whispered in Stephanie's ear. "Let's get out of here." Mark and Stephanie left Kierstein and the techno music thumping the space inside.

Outside the club, they kissed and groped each other some more.

"Let's go for a ride. I don't live far from here," Mark said.

Stephanie replied, "Okay," and Mark lead them to his white Dodge Charger. A few minutes into the ride, Stephanie said,

"I need to go home. Can you take me home?"

"Let's hang out a little while," Mark answered back. "I want to make sure you're alright."

The drinks had really hit Stephanie by then. Mark continued to drive. About 20 minutes later, they came to a stop at a house Mark rented with several other guys who attended DU.

"Where are we? I need to go home."

"Let's just go inside for a minute. I'll get you some water to help ease the morning hangover."

Mark got out of the car, walked around to the passenger side and opened the door for Stephanie. He grabbed her arm and helped her out of the car. They walked swaying a little and holding each other as they walked down the walkway and up the front steps.

"Are you gonna take care of me? You're a good guy?" Stephanie slurred.

"I'm gonna take care of you. Come on in."

As they entered, Mark helped Stephanie to the couch just to

the left of the door. "Wait here and I'll get you some water."

Mark returned about a minute later. Stephanie was lying down on the couch. He set the water on the coffee table in front of the couch and climbed onto the couch between her legs. Mark began lifting up Stephanie's shirt, kissing her stomach and working his way up.

"I have a boyfriend," Stephanie said in a slow drunken way.

He ignored her, raised up, and began kissing her neck and touching her chest. Stephanie let out a small groan, melting into his touch. Then she said,

"I can't. I have a boyfriend." She pulled her shirt down and started to push Mark off. Again, he ignored her, grabbing her wrists and holding them up above her head, pinned against the couch cushions. He laid down on her kissing her neck.

"No. Stop," she said louder. She struggled, twisting under his weight. While twisting, her thigh hit up against his groin.

"What the fuck!" Mark yelled, as he sat up in pain.

Stephanie managed to roll onto the floor and started to stand up. Just as her hands left the floor, he grabbed her from behind and carried her to his bedroom. There Mark raped Stephanie several different ways. She struggled at first, then just let go as it happened, crying quietly to herself. When he finished, he rolled off. Stephanie just lay there violated and feeling lower than she ever had in life, with his fluids leaking out of her. She lay there until morning came. Mark woke up to her sitting on the edge of the bed.

"I need to go home," is all Stephanie said to him. Her clothes were ripped, so Mark got her a pair of boxers and a t-shirt to wear before they left, and he dropped her off at her apartment.

Chapter 25

At the police station, Malcolm, Reggie and Cliff were all separated for questioning. A pair of homicide detectives spoke to all of them in turn. Malcolm was the last person to be questioned from the group. He shared the events exactly as he had seen them happen. However, he didn't offer up any information about his school project or the fact that he had been questioned by Special Agents.

After the questioning, Malcolm walked out into the lobby of the police station. There he saw Reggie and the DU head football coach talking with Mark Walker.

"Malcolm," said Professor Walker. "You holding up okay?"

"I'm fine. What about Cliff?"

Reggie turned towards Malcolm and shook his head solemnly. "They're gonna hold him Maw. They're charging him for manslaughter. He never should have had that gun in there."

"If he didn't have that gun in there, we could all be dead.

It's not right. It's just not right," Malcolm said.

"We're doing all we can. We've got a lawyer and already started a collection to continue representation to try to get him out," said Coach Sloan.

"Thank you for helping him," said Malcolm. They shook hands then Malcolm turned to Reggie. They hugged, both hurting from the situation Cliff was in. When they let go, Malcolm looked Reggie in the eyes.

"Thank you Reggie. Thank you. I don't know where I'd be if you and Cliff weren't with me. Let me know what I can do to help get Cliff out. He doesn't deserve this." Malcolm's eyes welled up with tears. Reggie continued to look into Malcolm's eyes.

"Take care of yourself brother. We'll stay in-touch." They embraced again, then Malcolm walked out with Professor Walker and got into his car.

They stopped at a diner just a few miles from the police station on their way back to Malcolm's college apartment. Over a cup of coffee and a hot meal, Malcolm filled Professor Walker in on the details of everything that had happened since he last saw him at the hospital in Atlanta. After their meal and discussion, Professor Walker dropped him off at his apartment where he stayed the night.

Chapter 26

Early the next morning Malcolm drove to Oakland on his way to Professor Temkin's house. As he approached the city that evening, traffic slowed until it finally came to a halt. He scanned the local channels until he came upon what was going on. The CA State Solidarity, a racist skinhead group, had come up into Oakland to counter-protest the Black Liberation Party, a black separatists group, who had convened to demonstrate against a recent shooting of a black male by a white male claiming self-defense. The white shooter had been released from further investigation and prosecution. Malcolm plugged Professor Temkin's address into the Waze travel app on his iPhone. It rerouted him along some back streets where he hoped to move past the congestion.

While traveling the side streets, he noticed that some of the demonstration had spread to the other areas within the city. He saw around 15 white members of what he assumed was the CA State Solidarity yelling and spitting at several black people as they walked nearby. Within a couple of minutes of harassing a black woman and what looked like her 4-year-old child and a baby, a group of 12 black men and teenagers emerged out of an apartment complex that she had walked into moments before. As the black mob walked to confront the white protestors, more blacks emerged from different areas around the block. Within what seemed like seconds, the CA State Solidarity was surrounded by about 30 black men and teenagers. A brawl ensued. Malcolm heard gunshots and the crowd dispersed. Two white men were on the ground and a black teenager hobbled away as if he'd been shot, or was at least seriously injured.

Malcolm turned right at the next street in order to get some distance from what was occurring before his eyes and from the potential bullets that could again start to fly. Traffic was still extremely slow moving on these back roads with cars parked haphazardly in the middle of the road. Malcolm saw two black teenagers running out of a store with cases of beer. They jumped into a car with another black man at the wheel. Malcolm drove down two more blocks and took a left. The mob had not gone this way. As Malcolm slowly drove, looking for trouble on both sides of the street, a figure burst out from an alley and right into the side of Malcolm's car. As the man hit his car, their eyes met. He had a shaved head and a tattoo of a swastika on the right side of his neck. Malcolm froze, not knowing what to do. The man was injured and bleeding. He left a large streak of blood across the hood of Malcolm's car before continuing to hobble down the street.

Malcolm sat stunned watching this situation unfold. After

the skin-head had passed Malcolm's car, he ducked behind a parked car to the right of Malcolm. He watched in wait for him to emerge again. As Malcolm looked to his left, he saw a group of 4 black men in their late teens or early twenties running towards him and up the alley where the white man had emerged from.

"Where he at?" one of the black men yelled to Malcolm. Malcolm sat there, still stunned.

"Where he at?" the man yelled again. Malcolm pointed up the street in the opposite direction of where the skin-head lay. The pursuers followed Malcolm's direction and slipped out of sight within a minute. Malcolm sat in his car still stunned at what had occurred. Why had he pointed them away from the skin-head?

Malcolm once had a run-in with a group of skin-heads as a teenager in Colorado Springs, which, if the police did not show up when they did, would not have ended well for him. He continued to sit there not sure of what to do. Without even really knowing what he was doing, he felt his hand move onto his car door handle. It felt like an out-of-body experience. In this dream-like state, he felt himself walking around the car the skin-head had ducked behind. The man was still there, lying on the ground in a small pool of his own blood. The white man said something to Malcolm, but he couldn't quite understand what was being said. He lay on his side, propped up on one elbow, looking at Malcolm. Malcolm moved closer.

"Why'd you do it man? I wouldn't have done that for a nigger. Why'd you do it?"

The man's head fell and Malcolm witnessed the skin-head's last breath leave his body.

Chapter 27

Malcolm arrived at Professor Temkin's house as dusk was coming on. It was not unlike the first time he pulled up to the professor's house. Malcolm felt an uneasy feeling as he remembered being attacked and waking up not knowing where he was that first night. This evening he was physically well, but emotionally aged. The experiences that he had undertaken since the last time he was here made him feel 10 years older. There was so much that he thought he knew just 6 months ago that he questioned and even doubted now. Malcolm thought about a scene in the *Matrix*. He had watched the movie with Keanu Reeves when it had been shown on TV and later purchased the book. In one particular scene, Morpheus, the leader of the rebellion against the computer generated artificial reality that keeps human minds imprisoned, offers Neo, a computer hacker identified as a potential savior in this rebellion, an option to take one of two pills after he was introduced to a part of the true reality. Morpheus says to Neo,

"You take the blue pill, the story ends. You wake up in your bed and believe whatever you want to believe. You take the red pill, you stay in Wonderland, and I show you how deep the rabbit hole goes." If given the choice, would Malcolm have chosen to have his eyes opened to truth or go about his life as so many others continue to go through life, blind, but not full of so much turmoil inside? Right now, he still didn't know truth. All he knew is that the world was much different now than it once was to him.

Professor Temkin greeted him at the door.

"Come in Malcolm. How are you holding up?"

"I'm hanging in there. There's a lot of action around here."

"Yeah, I've seen some of the skin-head rallies on the news. Did you see any of that coming in?" Malcolm smiled.

"What?" asked Professor Temkin.

"Yes, I saw it. It feels like this world is falling apart."

"It's not Malcolm. It's always been this way. There are a lot of blind people in this world. There always have been, but what's going on is making those who can't see, fall even more into darkness. At the same time, there are good people too and there are blind people gaining their sight every day. Malcolm was confused by this. Professor Temkin's attitude and even demeanor seemed to have changed so much from what he saw from him just weeks before.

"What's going on with you? You didn't even seem to want to be involved before?"

"You woke me up from my slumber, Malcolm. Thank you for that. There is more we can do. There are people out there that will be willing to help us. I not only hope it, I feel it."

"Then where do we go from here?" asked Malcolm.

"We find our friends working in areas targeted by this group and people with power or influence over the masses. From what I've been able to gather, anything under government control that has the ability to introduce a direct additive is being targeted by this group that is working to numb the American people. We need to find our friends in these places, including the Center for Disease Control *(CDC)* within departments dealing with vaccines, the National Pesticide Information Center *(NPIC)* and United States Environmental Protection Agency *(EPA)* working on water treatment and pesticide management."

Professor Temkin noticed Malcolm's eyes go large. "What is it?" he asked.

"Water Treatment facilities," Malcolm stated.

"Ok?" said Professor Temkin.

"I met a man just after he'd been in a car accident. He sent me to find his daughter to apologize for the racism he'd shown his son-in-law. I tracked her down. When I met with her, she had already separated from that man. His wife said that he used to be a great man, but then his work became too important, and he left their family."

Malcolm paused for a moment. "Bruce Dobson is his name. He works at a water treatment facility."

"His job was too important, or even more likely, too dangerous," stated Professor Tempkin.

"Exactly," Malcolm said.

Earlier that day, when Malcolm had gotten back in his car and drove on towards the professor's house, he had continued to think about what the white supremacist had said to him. *"Why did you do it? I wouldn't have done that for a nigger."* Malcolm didn't know why. What he did know is that he didn't hate the man. Not only did he not hate that man, he almost felt a connection, even a type of kinship that seemed totally irrational, given the situation. But, he could not deny what he felt. After arriving at Professor Temkin's house and talking with him, Malcolm left, checked into his motel and again started reminiscing on what had happened earlier that evening. While in bed, Malcolm sat up and wrote. He had once read a quote that resonated with him. He never really quite internalized why it resonated with him, until that moment.

"Enlightenment for a wave is the moment wave realizes that it is water. At that moment all fear of death disappears." – Thich Nhat Hanh. Malcolm contemplated his own faith and wrote the following:

"Does it unify or create separation? It takes many forms and wears many cloaks, but in its essence it is the same. The names of Hitler and the act of black slavery signify 'historical' prejudice in our modern American vernacular, but it continues to be alive and well today. Although many historical prejudices are outwardly rejected towards Jews, blacks, women, religion, and other groups considered minority or that share a 'protected' status, there still lives an underlying feeling of separation with some amongst us. . . including prejudice that some within these 'protected' groups demonstrate towards others. At the same time, other types of prejudice, like that towards same sex attraction, has morphed into more acceptable forms of separation with groups professing things like, 'we love the individual, but will not accept the homosexual act.' While judgment continues to be held due to the physical or psychological characteristics of a person, without the true realization of the deep connection that we all share, the enlightened and inner peaceful state that one may desire will continue to elude the person seeking it."

There were things that haunted Malcolm within his own religion. Historical restrictions for the priesthood amongst blacks, including degrading remarks from an early prophet of the church around "colored" people. Historical polygamy, where the prophet took many wives, some very young and some married to other men he had sent on missions for the church, also deeply bothered him. It was still taught that polygamy will occur within the "hereafter." He had chosen to look past the ideals that bothered him and embrace the good that is now, but recent events had shed even more light on those doctrines to Malcolm. What would he do? What he really believed, he didn't know. He just knew the uneasy feeling in his gut…deep within his belly. He would revisit this again, he thought, but now, he had more pressing things that needed his attention.

Chapter 28

Stephanie looked over towards her bedside dresser at her ringing mobile phone. It was Malcolm. When it stopped ringing, she turned it off, curled up in her bed and just cried. Stephanie spent the day in bed, drifting in and out of sleep between her sobbing. She only left her bed once that day to use the restroom. Around 5:00 PM, Clarissa, one of Stephanie's roommates, along with Nicki and Marci, knocked on her door. When Stephanie didn't answer, Clarissa slowly opened the door.

"Hey Steph, you okay?" she asked.

"I just don't feel well," answered Stephanie.

"You don't look very well. What can I get you?"

"Nothing" Stephanie paused, then said, "thank you though."

"You let me know if you need anything. I'll keep checking on you." Stephanie nodded her head and curled back into her pillow.

Later that night, Stephanie turned her phone back on. There were several messages from Malcolm. She didn't listen to them. Instead she just browsed social media: Facebook, Twitter, and Instagram. She saw the smiling faces and great accomplishments of people she knew in person and people she didn't know any other way but through social media. She looked at her own profile. She saw herself trying to portray the images that she saw everybody else highlighting, but as she looked at her pictures and her posts, it just felt fake. She wasn't the self-confident, happy person with a bright future those words and pictures attempted to make her out to be. She was an outsider and a loner on the inside. She envied the close relationships others around her seemed to have. She had once felt that real bond with her sister when they were younger, but that was gone now. She didn't even feel like she knew who her sister was anymore. *Why am I even trying?* she cried to herself.

Stephanie spent the next 4 days in bed. Getting up only briefly to go to the bathroom or get a little bit to eat from the kitchen. Clarissa, Nicki, and Marci all checked on her occasionally. Messages from Professor Walker now added to those from Malcolm. Still she refused to answer their calls. All she could think about was dying and escaping from the hell she lived within.

Chapter 29

"Please call me back. I just want to make sure you're okay. I love you," Malcolm said as he hung up the phone.

"Is everything okay?" asked Professor Temkin.

"I don't know. I just can't get ahold of Stephanie. I'm sure she's fine. Let's go."

Malcolm and Professor Temkin drove towards Synthia Dobson's house. When they pulled up, Tyson and Rex were out throwing a tennis ball with several other neighborhood kids in a type of keep-away game. When they approached Synthia's door, the two boys looked over towards them.

"Hi Tyson. Hi Rex," called Malcolm. The boys waved, said "hi" and went back to their game.

Malcolm knocked and Synthia opened the door. "Hello Ms. Dobson."

"Please, call me Synthia."

"Synthia, this is Edward Temkin." Professor Temkin stepped forward and shook her hand.

"It's a pleasure to meet you Synthia." Synthia nodded with a confused look on her face.

"I'm sorry to bother you again, but I wanted to see if you might be able to help us with something."

"Well, that depends on what it is," Synthia said with a smile. "Come on in."

They all sat down in her front room. Malcolm couldn't help but remember their last conversation and the wreck that had brought him there.

"Well, what is it that you two need?"

"We wanted to know if you could help us find Bruce."

Synthia sighed. "Bruce? Why do you want to find Bruce?"

Professor Temkin answered with, "Bruce works for the local water treatment plant, doesn't he?"

"He does," now directing her words towards Malcolm, she continued, "but as I told you Malcolm, we aren't together anymore. He's picked up and left all of us."

"There may be more to his work than he's been able to share with you. What did he tell you about what he does?" asked Malcolm.

"Well, he runs the county water treatment facility. He makes sure that it meets EPA standards and makes sure what needs to be added, is added."

Malcolm noticed a water dispenser container in the corner of the kitchen that was just visible from where he sat.

"Why do you have a water dispenser? It doesn't instill confidence in the water quality if the treatment facility manager's family won't drink it, does it?" Synthia was quiet for a second, as she thought.

"Bruce set up the service about a year and a half ago. We used to drink the tap water, but he insisted on it. And…well…it just stuck."

"Why did he insist on it?" asked Professor Temkin.

"I honestly don't know. Maybe it had to do the type of additives they started putting in, but I really don't know. All I know is that he insisted."

"Now I really don't mean to pry, but did you notice anything odd about Bruce before he left?" asked Professor Temkin.

"You mean besides turning into an asshole?" Synthia paused for a minute as if revisiting her memory of him.

"He used to be great with the kids and me. Then he took a promotion at work. His days at work started to get longer, and he just seemed to be on edge all the time. When he wasn't an asshole, he seemed to be in another world, like something was always on his mind. I asked him about it, but he just said he was thinking about a project at work. He wouldn't say more than that. I wondered if it was another woman, and I asked him about it. He denied it. Then, after a while, he just left."

Professor Temkin got the address of the water treatment facility, where Bruce worked, from Synthia.

"What is he driving, Synthia?" asked Malcolm. She described a blue Toyota pickup truck with an extended cab.

"I think it is a Toyota Tacoma," she said.

"Do you know where he lives?" asked Professor Temkin.

"No…well wait." Synthia got up from the couch and walked into what Professor Temkin and Malcolm assumed was her bedroom. She had a white envelope in her hand when she returned.

"He does send money every month. I assume the return address is where he lives." Synthia pointed to the return address on the envelope, then handed it to Professor Temkin. "You can have it. I don't need the envelope," Synthia said, as she watched the professor take out a pen to write the address down.

"Thank you. You have been a lot of help."

Later that day, Malcolm and Professor Temkin parked outside of the address Synthia had given them for Bruce Dobson, which was located about 10 miles from Synthia's home on the other side of the city. About 6:00 PM a blue Toyota pickup truck pulled into the driveway. They watched the tall black man get out of his truck and walk up to the front door of the house. Malcolm and the professor got out of their car and walked up the front pathway to Bruce's door. About 30 seconds after ringing the doorbell, Bruce opened the door.

"Can I help you?"

Both Malcolm and the professor introduced themselves. Malcolm played the role of a student researching the chemicals and additives used within sewage and potable water systems to create safe drinking water for the community it serves. After explaining this, Bruce looked like he was only half buying the story.

"So why are you here?,", he asked Professor Temkin.

"I've been a friend of Malcolm's for a while. He came to visit me and asked if I would like to tag along. In my past, I had researched chemical additives out of Stanford and was curious about how things have progressed here in the modern days." Professor Temkin smiled pleasantly as he finished his explanation.

Bruce stared at the professor slowly shaking his head. He seemed to see right through their story, but didn't call them on it. "So, what do you want to know?" he finally said.

"What is your role at the plant?" Malcolm asked.

"Well, I oversee the facility, ensure that the proper concentration of chemicals are added and that the water system remains free from external contaminants once within the system. I also ensure frequent testing through various ports within the system to ensure the integrity is fully maintained."

"What are the specific chemicals added to the water system?" Malcolm asked. Bruce listed off some standard chemicals and treatments utilized in the purification process. Malcolm glanced over at the professor. From the look on his face, the professor knew that Bruce was holding something back.

"Is that everything that's added?" Professor Temkin asked in a way that ensued the fact that he knew Bruce was holding back information. He looked back at Professor Temkin. It was silent for about 30 seconds, which seemed much longer than that, with a palpable tension in the air.

"Yep," Bruce finally answered.

Professor Temkin decided to go out on a limb and stated, "I was a scientist that worked on the implementation of Xonalin to the flu vaccine. I left my family after my son had been killed, which occurred when I tried to expose what was going on with these chemicals."

"What exactly do these chemicals do?" Bruce asked.

Professor Temkin explained the emotional numbness that these agents have been shown to create.

"Last week I was contacted by an individual from the office of the Environmental Protection Agency. They asked me to contact them should anyone unusual start hanging around the facility that should not be there, especially if they come asking about the chemicals added to the water supply," Bruce said.

Fear shot through Malcolm. He looked over at Professor Temkin, who maintained a calm knowing focus on Bruce.

"Are you going to let them know about us?" asked Professor Temkin.

Bruce said, "They told me that there were people who were part of a terrorist sect that would try to gain knowledge to help enable them to attack our water systems."

Bruce sat silent after his statement. Malcolm looked back towards Professor Temkin, who maintained his calm gaze on Bruce.

"Are you going to tell them about us?" Malcolm asked. Bruce looked Malcolm in the eyes.

"No. I'm going to help you."

Bruce knew more than Malcolm or the Professor had known. Beyond overseeing the local chemical additives, he had worked with other treatment facilities across the nation to initiate programs and ensure others were placed in charge of those facilities that would follow direction without second guessing the protocols and chemicals being introduced to the water way.

"When this started, something just didn't feel right. From my office computer, I searched specific chemicals that were newly introduced to my Water Treatment Facility. I found some controversial research on the additives. As I read through some of the articles, my computer basically shut down. When I was able to get it restarted, the website I had been on before was blocked from my system. All that would come up was an error code. Within 10 minutes, I received a call from the Officer of Water for the EPA in Washington DC. The next morning, they had me on a flight there to meet with him."

"What did he say?" Malcolm asked.

"He fed me full of a bunch of prepared jargon that I knew was said to hide something. He must have sensed it, because then it got serious. He said, 'Bruce, let me make this clear. The wellbeing of not just you, but also your family is very closely tied with the confidentiality and compliance of the things we have discussed. Am I clear?' I could see the coldness in his eyes. After I arrived home, my family had a surprise for me. While I had been gone, an agent from the CIA had visited my oldest son's school. After talking about what he did, he mentioned other systems that they work to protect. The water treatment facilities were one. This agent told the class that my son's father was a hero that did all of the things required of him to keep the water safe for his community and his family. Before he left, he handed Tyson an envelope to give to me when I returned home that night."

Bruce stood up and walked into another room. When he came back, he held a piece of paper in his hand. He gave it to Professor Temkin. The Professor read it aloud.

"*Dear Bruce, Thank you for your willingness to maintain the compliance and full confidentiality of the work the EPA is performing within the United States water ways. As you know, the only way the safety and security of your family will be ensured is through the ultimate adherence to these principals. Sincerely, Agent Sikes, Central Intelligence Agency, United States Government.*

After that, I ordered water to be delivered to my home. I couldn't have my family drinking the water we treated. A few more times, I would see Agent Sikes at different places. I walked past him one day as I picked my son up from school. Another time

I saw him while I was buying groceries near where I lived. Each time, he made a point to ensure that I saw him."

"That's when you left your family," said Professor Temkin knowingly. Bruce nodded his head yes.

"It's the only way I could protect them. To make the agency believe that they were no longer important to me."

"From what I've been able to gather, and it's only been in pieces, is that what's going on had to do with 4 F-words, flu, fluoride, flies (mosquitos and fruit flies), and fundamentalists. In most of the documents I've seen these are referred to as F-1, F-2, F-3, and F-4. I found out what these stood for by mistake. This has been kept pretty confidential," Bruce said. Professor Temkin commented and asked a question,

"We've gathered flu, fluoride, and flies, but tell us more about fundamentalists. What do you mean?"

"Fundamentalist, the ones you hear about on the news at times. Extreme religious zealots like Warren Jeffs. It also includes hate groups, like the KKK, skin heads, and black panthers. At times, these groups get out of hand and diverge from the influence the government wants. That's when you see them make mainstream news. And, that is when they're occasionally taken down by the federal government. But even more of a focus than these extremist groups are the mainstream religious institutions. I heard on one occasion that fundamentalists, fundamentally further the work. I didn't know what it meant at first, but it stuck with me."

Chapter 30

Malcolm lay in the motel bed, unable to sleep, thinking about their conversation with Bruce earlier in the day. What Professor Walker told him also circled in his head. He couldn't get ahold of Stephanie either, but he had approached one of her roommates on campus who confirmed that she was okay before he left for California. What was going on with her? Why was she avoiding him?

Malcolm got up from bed and walked shirtless and barefoot outside, in a pair of workout shorts. He looked up and saw the full moon. As a child he had spent many nights sleeping in the back yard, just staring at the night sky. Part of it spoke to him, saying that what you think you are and what you are experiencing now, is just a tiny part of what actually is. He felt an escape from his pain in that night sky. As he gazed at the moon and the stars as a child, it provided a brief relief from the anxiety and fear he felt back then from the pain over the abuse he had endured. It seemed like the only nights that falling asleep didn't mean reliving his abuse over and over again, were the ones where he fell asleep gazing at the beauty and wonder within that night sky. A world that provided hope and a greater plan. It was beyond what he could conceptualize in his mind, but he felt it, and it felt good.

"Hey good lookin." Malcolm turned around. That break in the silence surprised him and broke him out of his trance. Malcolm looked at the black woman approaching him. Behind her were two small children.

"Momma, I'm tired," the smallest, a little girl said. She looked to be around 4 years old. Her older brother, probably only 5 or 6 years old, just stood there looking at Malcolm. The woman ignored her child.

"You want some company?" she said as she came closer and pressed up against him. Malcolm pushed her arms down off his lower hips where she had placed them.

"Your children are tired. Take them home," Malcolm said.

"They're fine. I'll take care of you real nice," she said as she grabbed his hand to place on her breast, while touching his groin with her other hand. Malcolm stepped back.

"Your kids need a fucking mother. Start acting like one!" Malcolm shouted.

"Take your sister to the room Rajan." The older brother took his sister's hand and they walked to a motel room 4 doors down.

"I'll suck you for $20. I'll fuck you for $30 and do

anything for $50. What do you want?"

"I want you to start acting like a fucking mother and take care of those kids! They deserve more than this!" A man stepped out of the shadows at the end of the motel walkway. He walked aggressively towards where Malcolm and the woman stood.

"I told you to leave your fucking kids bitch!"

The woman looked at Malcolm as the man kept moving forward. The man grabbed her by the arm. She yanked her arm away as he did this, and he hit her on the side of her face with an open hand. She fell to one knee and put her hands up over her face, as if to protect herself for more blows to come.

Malcolm stepped forward and hit the man as hard as he could with a heavy right hand. The man stumbled back. Malcolm then kicked him as hard as he could in the groin. This pitched his face down and towards Malcolm. Malcolm grabbed the back of his head with both hands, forcing it down to his knee, which came up to deliver a solid blow, exploding the man's nose. He dropped to the ground. Malcolm jumped on top, beating him over and over again. All the pain, all the hurt, came through with each strike he threw. He felt someone hitting him from behind. He jumped off the now still body lying on the ground.

"Get the fuck off him," the woman said as she continued forward swinging her arms. Malcolm put his forearms up to guard his face, and at his first opening, he shoved her to the ground.

"Your kids deserve more than this!" Malcolm yelled leaning over her.

"He's gonna kill me!" she yelled back. Malcolm turned back towards the man lying still on the ground and kicked him hard in the gut.

"Get up!" Malcolm said to the woman, who was just sitting on the ground with her arms around her knees.

"Get up!" He grabbed her left arm with his right hand and lead her over to the door her children had gone into.

"Start acting like a fucking mother," he said in a low stern voice. "Your kids deserve so much more than this."

She was crying now. The woman pulled a room key from the small bag she was carrying and went inside. Malcolm turned back towards his room. The man was gone. All that was left was the small pool of blood where his face once laid, with spattered drops of blood around that area. Malcolm went back into his motel room, then shut and locked the door with the deadbolt and chain. He got back in his bed, mind reeling from what had just happened. It all seemed like a dream. After moving restless for an hour or so in bed, he eventually drifted off to sleep.

The loud bang woke Malcolm from sleep. He sat up in bed. Did he just hear what he thought he heard? His heart started pounding. He pulled the drapes back just a crack and saw a black man running past his room down the motel walkway. Malcolm's heart felt like it fell right out of his chest. He stood there for a moment, probably a full minute, then unlocked his door and took off the chain. It had just started to become light. He looked down the corridor in the direction he saw the man running from just a few moments earlier. Malcolm again checked in the direction the man ran towards. He wasn't anywhere to be seen. Malcolm looked back the other way, towards the woman's room. The door was a quarter of the way open. Malcolm jogged towards the door and opened it the rest of the way. Inside, the two children were crying, trying to wake their mother. She lay motionless on the floor with a deep red spot in the center of her chest. Blood had started to pool around her body.

"Come with me," he told the kids, "I'm going to call someone to help your mom." He didn't know why he said that. He knew she was dead, but it was all that came to his mind at that moment. Malcolm took the kids to his room and dialed 911. While waiting for the police to arrive, he tried to calm the children.

"What is your name sweetheart?"

"Ryan," the little girl said, still with tears rolling down her face.

"Ryan, that's a beautiful name. What were you all doing out here?"

"Mom was working," answered Rajan.

Malcolm kept the conversation going to keep the kids' minds off of what had just happened. He asked them about what they like to do, where they lived, and if they had other family that they knew of. Rajan liked playing basketball. Ryan liked to dance. They told Malcolm that they used to have a grandmother, but she went to live in heaven.

About 15 minutes later, the police arrived. Malcolm told

them what had happened that morning, leaving out the activities from the night before.

"What's going to happen to these kids?" Malcolm asked the police officers.

One of the two officers standing there answered, "We'll check to see what other family they have. If they have any we can track down, we'll see if they are willing and fit to take care of these kids." Two more police cruisers pulled up.

"What if you can't find family to take care of them?"

"Then we will place them with Child Protective Services, and they will look for a foster home to place them in," the same officer answered.

"I need to know what happens to these kids." The officer took Malcolm's information down, gave him the number for the police department and the number to the local Child Protective Services department. He told Malcolm to call in a week or two, to give them time to sort out their family situation.

Malcolm went back into his room where the children sat on his bed watching TV. The second police officer followed him in, while the one who had answered Malcolm's questions met up with the other officers at the scene of the crime.

"Rajan, Ryan," Malcolm said. "These men are going to take care of you, okay?" Rajan looked at Malcolm and nodded his head, affirming that he understood. Ryan just kept watching the cartoons Malcolm had turned on for them.

"I'm also going to make sure that you and your little sister are taken care of, okay?" Rajan nodded again. "I'm going to come find you in a week or two to check on you and make sure everything is okay. Everything is going to be okay." Ryan kept watching the TV.

"Okay, Ryan? I'm going to come find you to make sure that you're taken care of. I'll even bring some toys, okay?" Her eyes got big.

"You're gonna bring some toys?" she asked.

"Yeah, in a week or two, okay?"

"Okay" and she smiled. Malcolm gave each of them a hug and proceeded to pack up his belongings. The officers took the kids to their patrol car. One of the women police officers who had come in one of the last two cruisers to the scene, spoke to the children and tried to comfort them. Malcolm grabbed his suitcase, walked outside and gave each of the kids one more hug.

"Remember the toys; I'm going to bring you some." Ryan smiled, Rajan maintained the blank look on his face.

"Everything is going to be okay." Malcolm turned towards his car, got in, and drove away.

Chapter 31

Malcolm drove through the day and into the night. It took 18 hours, plus the bathroom breaks and quick stops at fast food drive-throughs along the way. Malcolm bought a can of Copenhagen to help him keep his eyes open during the drive. Like coffee, this was something that he hadn't done since his teenage years and was another act in direct opposition to the teachings of the church that he had adhered to just weeks before. As he made this conscious decision, he almost felt liberated, as if he was taking a bit of himself back.

Malcolm pulled up to Stephanie's apartment at 7:42 the next morning. Seven forty-two was an interesting number. Malcolm remembered reading the significance of that within the Christian faith. Seven, signifying 7 years of the New World being under the control of Satan. The covenant made with the anti-Christ, would appear to provide peace for the first half of 7 years. But during the second 42 months, Satan would betray Israel and do all in his power to ensure their destruction. All good and pure will seem lost to the masses. It will appear as if Satan has won. As Malcolm watched his car clock, it clicked over to 7:43. After that final 42 month period, Jesus would return, where he is supposed to reign for 43 months. While here, Jesus is prophesied to rid the world of Satan's evil and the thoughts that he had planted within everyone's mind.

Malcolm pondered those thoughts for a moment, then got out of his car and walked up the stairs to Stephanie's apartment. He knocked on the door. One of Stephanie's roommates answered.

"Hi, is Stephanie here?"

"Um, let me check," the young lady answered. As she turned to go check, Malcolm went in and headed straight to Stephanie's bedroom.

"Hey, I said I would check," the roommate said more forcefully. Malcolm ignored her and proceeded to open Stephanie's door.

"Steph?" The roommate was right behind Malcolm.

"I told him to wait and I would check to see if you were available."

"It's okay," answered Stephanie. Malcolm walked over to her bed and sat on the edge. He saw a bottle of pills on her bedside dresser.

"Are you doing okay?" asked Malcolm. Stephanie pulled him over to her and touched his groin. She closed her eyes and touched her breast. As she did this the blanket moved to the side, exposing the lower half of her body. She wasn't wearing any panties. Her hand moved down to her own groin area.

"Fuck me," Stephanie said, still with her eyes closed.

"The door's still open," said Malcolm. Stephanie pulled him to her again.

"Fuck me."

In a different circumstance, Malcolm may have felt differently about her request, but something was terribly off. Malcolm knew it and could feel it as clearly as he had felt anything. He pulled back, pulled the blanket over the lower half of her body, stood up and shut the door.

"Why haven't you answered any of my calls?" Malcolm asked.

"I don't even turn you on anymore. Are you embarrassed of me?" she said.

"Are you okay?" asked Malcolm.

"No, I wanted you in me. Why don't you want me?" Malcolm leaned in towards Stephanie and started kissing her, on the mouth, the neck, and down to her breast. Stephanie moaned. Malcolm took off his shirt and pants and they continued to make out with Malcolm on top of her. Stephanie pushed him to the side and got on top of him. Anxiety continued to escalate inside of Malcolm. *Something is terribly wrong*, continued to echo in his head. Stephanie got off of Malcolm, frustrated that he was not excited enough to engage in sex and turned to her side.

"I don't even turn you on," she said again.

"You do turn me on, but something's going on. I've never

seen you act like this."

"That's why I never act like this! You only want it when I act like a little proper school girl. I have needs too."

"You don't answer my calls. You don't return my calls. What's going on?" yelled Malcolm.

"You mean besides the world around me falling apart?" she shot back. Malcolm looked again at the bottle on the night stand. He picked it up. It was an old prescription of Percocet.

"Have you been taking these?"

"Are you judging me?" Stephanie shot back. She then got up, put some shorts on and walked out of her room. Malcolm set the pill bottle back down on the bedside dresser. Stephanie's phone was there. He picked it up, typed in the phone screen password that he had seen her type a 1000 times. He looked at her text messages and his heart sank. He scrolled through several dialogues she had had with several men. Each one talked about intimate acts they would perform together. Sexy and seductive pictures were also exchanged on two of the threads.

"What are you doing?" Malcolm looked up and saw Stephanie standing at the door.

"What the fuck is this? Are you fucking around with other guys?"

"You leave me alone. What do you expect me to do?"

"I didn't expect you to fuck around with other guys! What happened to you wanting me all to yourself? What the fuck are you doing?"

"You knew this would never work. I'm just your little white girlfriend for a minute. You told me about other girls you've fucked."

"Not since I've been seeing you! What the fuck is going on with you?"

"We're not compatible. You want me to be your little white princess. I have needs too!"

"Do you realize these guys don't give a shit about you? All they want is a piece! Is that what you want?"

"You don't know what they want! They are there for me when you're not."

"Fuck you! I was gone for a few days! You don't even answer the goddamn phone when I call!" There was a brief pause.

"Nobody has ever said fuck you to me, and you think I should love you? Get out!"

"Fuck you, Stephanie!" Malcolm walked out of the room, left the apartment and got in his car.

Chapter 32

Malcolm's mind was reeling. He could visualize Stephanie falling for and giving herself in every way, to men who had no real respect for her. What is going on with her? Why can't she see it? He wanted to try to understand, but when he spoke to her, he couldn't even recognize the presence that came from Stephanie. She was distant, bitter, and full of disdain towards him. He knew that she was hurting. It was as if she was blind, looking for love everywhere but where it actually might be. He wanted to care for that person behind the pain, behind the lies, and behind the betrayal that now seemed to encapsulate her, but how could he do it like this? He couldn't. It hurt too much.

Malcolm's mind kept running a thousand thoughts a minute. He couldn't believe what had just happened. Something was going on deep inside of her. He knew that it was beyond him. Maybe the stress of the situation. Maybe the need to escape from the reality that they were uncovering. He didn't know for sure. Again, part of him wanted to go back into her room with kindness and really try to help. The other part of him wanted to walk away from this woman who had betrayed everything that meant something in their brief romantic relationship. Malcolm put a dip of Copenhagen in his mouth, stopped by a gas station where he filled up his car and bought two 40s of Miller High Life. The drive back from California was the first time Malcolm had chewed since in high school, and these two 40s of beer would be the first ones he would drink since that time. He drove towards a spot where he'd spent time thinking before. It was just outside of the city, a place surrounded by trees, with a small stream running through. It was a place he could be alone and feel closer to God then any church he'd ever attended.

When he got to the spot, he pulled into a dirt pull-off, shut off the car, grabbed the 40s and walked about 400 yards up a narrow dirt trail to an area with a sitting log and a small rock circle he had constructed a couple years ago for fire. This was his secret place. It reminded him of the place Winston first met a woman to make love to, in the classic novel *1984*. He had been studying it in a literature course that he took as one of his general requirements at DU. The government, also known as "Big Brother" constantly monitored the public through cameras and microphones that they used to keep the general population in line. A bit of wilderness was the first place that Winston really discovered he could be himself without fear of government recourse. This was Malcolm's special place…away from all who could watch or judge him, yet close enough to the city that he could get here quickly without having to take gear to camp with.

Malcolm sat on the ground with his back leaning against the log. He set one of the 40s beside him and cracked the lid on the other. Just the taste of Miller High Life in this place seemed to help him remember himself. He felt like his true self, away from expectations that others had for him. He suddenly felt more present than before he had gotten there. Malcolm thought back and remembered a time he had taken two of his friends and 3 girls to a spot like this, just outside of Colorado Springs. They built a fire and drank for a couple of hours, laughing and talking. In addition to beer, one of Malcolm's buddies brought a whisky flask with him. When it came time to leave and Malcolm stood up, the world started spinning around him. "Go ahead," he told the others, "I've got to piss." After his friends started back towards their cars, Malcolm did more than piss. He leaned over and vomited from the extra-large gulps of whisky he had consumed as the flask was handed around.

While leaning over and trying to gather himself, he heard voices yelling. Not in an excited drunk fun sort of way, but in an angry challenge. Malcolm wiped his mouth and watering eyes with his sleeve and started jogging down the trail. When he got near to where his truck was parked, he saw a stand-off between his friends and about 10 guys that he later found out came from a neighboring rival high school. They were on top of a small grass knoll making crude remarks to the girls and a couple even threw rocks at his friends in order to taunt them.

"Is that your truck?" one of the troublemakers said. Nobody responded.

"Fuck your truck!" The boy threw a rock in the direction of the truck, and the boys on the knoll all laughed.

These boys came from the privileged part of town. They were all excited about causing trouble when they had an unfair advantage, but they didn't know where Malcolm and his friends had come from. Malcolm and his buddies went to a high school that took in the kids who had been kicked out of every other local school. There were a couple of well-to-do families, but the majority were not, and their high school had its fair share of gangs, knives, and guns that made their way in. Many of the kids that started trouble at Malcolm's school felt like they had nothing to lose, coming from broken and even abusive homes. That would not be the case here. The more your opponent has to lose, the easier they are to convince that the conflict isn't worth it.

Malcolm quickly went to his truck where he always kept a baseball bat for situations like this. He unlocked his Toyota truck, grabbed the bat and jogged straight at the boys on the knoll. Malcolm's two friends followed his lead, with one grabbing a stick and the other grabbing a fist-size rock. They also started up the small grass hill. Malcolm remembered the fuzzy figures before him, while the world continued to spin around him. He hit the first boy he came to across his left side and arm, cracking two ribs and severely bruising his arm. The boy went down in pain and Malcolm focused on the others, who quickly backed out of reach.

Within a minute or two the rival boys had all gotten to their cars and took off soon after. Malcolm feared repercussions, either from police or from a group of boys from that school, but neither happened. It all just ended that night.

Another thought about that night entered Malcolm's mind. A month or two after that night on the trail, one of his friends who was with him that evening, Dave Ryan, told Malcolm that Malcolm's girlfriend, Anna (one of the girls they took with them), French kissed him after they left Malcolm vomiting on the trail. He remained friends with Dave, but ended the relationship with Anna.

Malcolm thought about those boys he had taken after with the bat. He thought that most if not all of those kids, probably were not bad. Each person needs a group or a face to relate to and embrace. Most act differently in groups than they would ever act alone. Sometimes, there is courage to do more good. Other times, it's engaging in activities to belong and be part of the group, even if it means hurting another that they would never hurt while alone.

Malcolm remembered studying the Bystander Effect in one of his Sociology classes. There were instances where 20 or more people stood around and watched an innocent person being brutally assaulted, where nobody stood up and helped. Most people just wait for someone else to act. Our innate need to connect with others and to belong or not stand out can often serve as a prison in situations like that.

Malcolm thought about the book *1984* again and some of

the tactics that the government, "Big Brother," used to maintain control. Sex and other indulgences were prohibited. Censorship was enforced. Without any of these releases, people grasped onto what it was they had left…the dysfunctional system of Big Brother. Malcolm couldn't help but think that it is not unlike alcoholics, drug abusers, workaholics, those that compulsively exercise or eat, and even the excitement of constant affairs with new people…everything that becomes an addiction. When people feel that they have nothing left, they grasp onto what they know, no matter how destructive or unhealthy it may be.

Malcolm thought about the religion he was raised in. He had grasped onto it when he felt there was nothing else…as his demons entered his mind and thoughts. He did not see the glaring control they exhibited back then, but he could see it now. Shaming and blaming by the church had become a culture of its members. In fact, a girlfriend of his had stopped going to church around the age of 12, after a Sunday lesson on sexual purity. The lesson displayed a beautiful red rose to signify the pure woman. Another rose, dead, wilted, brown, with leaves falling off, signified a girl who engaged in sexual relations before marriage. This girl had been sexually abused since the age of 6 by some older boys in the neighborhood. From that lesson, all she had learned was that she was like the dead, brown, and wilted rose and was not worth much in this world. This was the same girl that Malcolm had been with the night he confronted the group of boys taunting them on the hill. Malcolm didn't see it clearly when he felt the betrayal of her kissing his friend back then, but he understood more as he contemplated it now. She had still struggled with her worth, and thus acted from that perception of herself.

While reading about the Spanish conquest of Latin America, Malcolm read about the churches filled with gold, while so many starved within the city. Only the wealthy, or in their words, the "truly faithful" were allowed past the entryway of these churches. When Malcolm told others at church about this, people were abhorred at the thought of that. Malcolm had expected a different reaction. He expected them to see the similarity in what their church does with elaborate temples, with only the truly faithful able to enter the doors. A key criteria to entering their temple was again the full tithe of 10% of all income, along with sexual purity, abstinence from tobacco and alcohol, and never speaking or engaging with groups that speak out against the church. The full trifecta included the elimination of outlets, requirement of pay, and censorship amongst its members. Malcolm didn't share his thoughts with the other members of his church, but it did plant a seed within him that had added to his slow withdrawal from their congregation.

When Malcolm's mind was open to considering other potential truths, outside of what his church taught, he researched his religion further. He found out about the fact that blacks could not receive the "priesthood" until 1978. The priesthood was an advancement within the church that was given to boys as young as 12 years old. In 1852, the president of the church at the time,

Brigham Young, stated that, "any man having one drop of the seed of Cain [meaning black lineage] …in him cannot hold the priesthood and if no other Prophet ever spake it before I will say it now in the name of Jesus Christ I know it is true and others know it." Later he also stated, "The Lord had cursed Cain's seed with blackness and prohibited them the Priesthood." In regards to interracial marriages, he said, "If the white man who belongs to the chosen seed mixes his blood with the seed of Cain, the penalty, under the law of God, is death on the spot. This will always be so."

As times in the United States changed, the overwhelming prejudice against other races was not publicly acceptable, so new targets were focused on. Most recently, it had been the war on homosexual behavior. With the release of *The Proclamation of the Family* from the church, specifically denoting that God only accepts the marriage between a man and a woman, the movement began to gain steam. Throughout the United States, Mormons and other Christian organizations funded huge political movements to ban same-sex marriage. Homosexuals have become an acceptable target with leaders stating things like, "we accept them as people, but God cannot accept homosexual behavior."

Why would they do this? Malcolm thought. Their movement was not just directed towards their own true believers, but it was directed to the population at large. This instigated separateness, a feeling of superiority to another group and helped to create the environment that Malcolm's parents were caught up in…the absolute horror in uncovering that they had a gay son. This, despite the fact that things like plural marriage were preserved for the very faithful men of their faith. Polygamy was later "abolished here on earth," but was confirmed that it would resume in the hereafter. Joseph Smith, the founder and Prophet of the church, not only took on multiple wives, but included with that group a girl as young as 14 and those who were married to men he had sent away on missions.

The pattern of elimination of outlets, requirement of pay, and censorship amongst its members was not isolated to his particular religion. It was prominent in many that he studied while comparing and contrasting his own religion to others, but his religion was the one he knew best and the one he felt had betrayed him. These ideals were not any longer in isolation to his religious experiences. The pattern was also prevalent in what he saw happening now as he tried to uncover what was going on all around him, with the government he had once trusted.

Malcolm got up off of the ground, having only consumed one 40. He grabbed the other one and headed back to his car. It was time for him to head to the mountains--the place where he felt more clarity than anywhere on earth. That was his church and his religion.

When he got to his apartment, he threw some food in a bag, grabbed a sleeping bag, a small tent, a Coleman stove, some camouflage clothing, his Buck knife, and his Hoyt compound bow. When in his truck he started his 11 hour drive towards Northern

Arizona. Northern Arizona held a special place in Malcolm's heart. As a young boy, he was introduced to the area by his grandfather whose childhood home was there.

During Malcolm's childhood and up through is teenage years, he seemed to have constant anxiety in him. His special place, outside of his teenage home in Colorado Springs and especially the mountains in Northern Arizona, provided solace. He forgot about his problems while riding horseback through the ponderosa-pine-laden mountaintops there. Clear fresh air and an unbelievable clear night sky stimulated all of his senses on these trips. Malcolm and his grandfather would spend several days at a time during his summer visits, sleeping underneath the stars in their sleeping bags. Malcolm would look at the milky way, constellations, and shooting stars as they would streak across the night sky, while listening to his grandfather tell stories about his youth and how it was growing up there as a boy. His grandfather's family didn't have much money for entertainment, so his grandfather and his grandfather's brothers spent a lot of their time playing in Mother Nature's playground in the hills around them. As a result, nobody knew that area better than Malcolm's grandfather and his siblings.

Chapter 33

After driving through what was left of the afternoon and into the night on Hwy 40, through parts of New Mexico and into northeast Arizona, Malcolm arrived at a small town with an outfitters shop. He would stop here and sleep until morning, where he would buy an over-the-counter Arizona deer archery tag. Most of the hunts for big game in Arizona are through the lottery system, in order for the Department of Fish and Game to clearly monitor the size of the herds, but archery was a different story, at least for deer. Except for a few hunting units, which had the lottery system for archery as well, the odds of filling a tag for an average archery hunter was slim, ranging from 6-14% for those who purchased licenses.

Malcolm picked up archery early in his teens to ensure the opportunity to get out and hunt every year. As he spent more and more time using a bow for large game, he fell in love with it. He felt connected to the land and the animals around him. Everything with a bow takes place up close, which means you had to blend in and become a part of your surroundings, which is an entirely different experience than using a rifle. Malcolm laid his car seat down and fell asleep.

The next morning, he purchased his tag and drove up into an area he knew well. This was the place he and his younger brother hunted as teenagers. He hadn't been up here since the fall of his senior year in high school. His brother was alive and with him then. Malcolm was 17 that fall. His brother Jamin was just two years younger. They worked as a high-functioning team on those hills. With deer being most active during the early mornings and just before dark, Malcolm and Jamin spent those early mornings and evenings "glassing," or using binoculars to look over the hillsides for deer.

After watching the deer for a day or two, Malcolm and Jamin would deploy one of two tactics. The first would be a spot and stalk strategy, where one would stay put with the binoculars, watching the deer and directing the other with hand signals on where to go, when to stop, and when to look for the movement of an approaching deer. Sometimes this process would take hours, depending on the route the stalker had to take. The direction of the wind and cover were key elements to consider in this situation.

With an incredible sense of smell, a small breeze in the wrong direction would send the deer running in the opposite direction. The deer are also keenly aware of their surroundings, and any unnatural movement would alert the deer to a potential threat. Sometimes, Malcolm or Jamin would belly crawl through the long grass and slowly shuffle around trees and shrubs to get within arrow shot. At times, it would mean sitting still for 30 minutes and then only moving 3-4 feet before having to stop again. In order to ensure a well-placed shot through both lungs, Malcolm and his brother worked on getting within 40 yards.

Patience was the key. In order to get a clean pass through both lungs, it meant waiting for a broadside, or close to broadside angle, before releasing the arrow. There were other areas to target for a clean kill, but the margin of error went down significantly when shooting right for the heart or the carotid neck arteries. This spot and stalk strategy was almost exclusively deployed in the mornings, when they had all day to stalk the deer after it bed down for the day.

The second tactic was to identify the likely path of the animals. Deer, unlike elk, are very habitual. They tend to stay in the same general area to feed, drink, and bed, with little discrepancy on the path they traveled to each. After studying the habits of the deer from a good distance for a day or two, when they felt they could be fairly certain of a pattern, they would make themselves part of the surrounding area near the game trail or waterhole the deer frequented. In the morning, they would set out to arrive at their chosen spot for ambush at least 30 minutes before the first glimpse of light. For an evening ambush, they would arrive at least 2 hours before dusk.

The closest buck they took was at about 5 yards, when the deer practically walked right past them. The furthest they had taken a deer was at 65 yards, where short grass surrounding the buck from the front and the direction of the breeze prevented another angle of approach.

Shortly after their last hunt, Jamin was killed in a truck accident. He had grabbed a ride from school with one of his friend's older brothers. His buddy's brother drove a pickup truck. Jamin and a few others jumped in the bed of the truck. On the way home the brother took a shortcut on some dirt roads. As teenage boys will do sometimes, he tried to jostle his little brother's friends by swerving side-to-side, laughing at the boys tumbling around the back of the pickup, while they cursed loudly back at him. During one swerve, the tires skid on the dirt road then caught on a rock, which caused the truck to roll. All of the boys were thrown from the bed. The truck rolled and landed on the chest of Jamin. The boys got him back in the truck and raced towards the hospital, but Jamin never woke up from that incident. Physicians said he died on the way to the hospital from massive internal bleeding.

While trying to deal with the loss of his best friend and brother, Malcolm found himself depressed and reeling emotionally. He questioned life and our purpose here on earth. Since the summer before Malcolm's sophomore year in high school, his activity in church had waned. He was more interested in having some beers with friends and getting as far as he could with girls he met, than he was in going to church or living up to the principles they taught. At Jamin's funeral and again soon after, the church bishop had asked Malcolm,

"Do you want to see your brother again?"

"Yes," he had answered.

The Bishop continued, "There is only one way and it is through the Gospel of Jesus Christ, where families can be together forever. In order to have this, you must get yourself worthy to go through the LDS temple to receive the saving ordinances they provide there."

Stricken with grief and with the hope for a relationship with Jamin beyond this life, Malcolm re-engaged in church services and gave up drinking, tobacco, and sex. As he thought back now, he felt anger towards the bishop and other leaders within the church that leveraged a tragic situation to sway the actions of their flock.

Malcolm had never felt closer to God in the congregations of the church than he did while being engulfed within nature, far from any building built for worship. The church buildings, and especially the temple felt awkward and contrived. But, out of hope and after being told, "What if it's true? If it's true and you choose a different route in life, there will be nothing to bind you and your brother after this life. Be obedient to the principles and ordinances of the gospel for Jamin and your family," he was diligent in keeping the covenants the church asked him to keep.

Recent study and observation had taught him so much more of the church's tainted past. He saw the shame and blame it inflicted on others. He saw the division it created amongst ethnic and social groups. And, just as Stephanie's father had said to her years before, any religion dictating a liaison between him and God could never be a true religion. He didn't need a prophet or bishop to tell him what he must do. He felt God and that connection deep inside himself. Grief and fear had buried that, but now Malcolm felt that feeling grow.

When Malcolm got to his camp spot, he set up his tent, rolled out the sleeping bag inside, put on his camouflage and headed towards the tallest hill near him. He had seen many bucks around that area in the past. This area was a mix of tall ponderosa pine with juniper, sagebrush, and prickly pear cactus spread throughout the more open areas. Malcolm and his brother loved this area, because it had the perfect balance of deep forest and sparse topography that allowed them to feel engulfed within the trees and grasslands around them, yet open enough to allow strong visibility from the top of the surrounding peaks.

As he approached the base of the west side of the hill, he veered to the left. After following the ravine crevice on the north side of the mountain, he walked up on the seep, which trickled water, just as he had remembered it. Malcolm studied the moist ground around the seep. He saw doe, fawn, and buck tracks that had been left when they came to drink. Also within the mud, he saw what looked like coyote and raccoon tracks. This seep provided an opportunity during early morning hours and just before dark when the animals are more active. Malcolm looked up to the northern ridge and glanced over the game trails that made their way down. He started up the one that looked most used, with the easiest passage up the steep terrain.

Halfway up, Malcolm stopped. He saw the fresh prints of a cougar in the soft ground in front of him. He felt a panic spread through his body and his lungs seemed void of oxygen. This was his first time alone in this country. Memories of his brother came flooding in. No matter what, they always had each other's back. Knowing that had always provided peace, even in their youthful years. As long as they had each other, they could handle anything that came at them here and at home.

But, they no longer had each other. Jamin was gone. Malcolm was alone. Images flashed through his mind of following the blood trail long into the night from one of the bucks Jamin had shot. A storm had lurked throughout most of the day, but it came in quickly as darkness fell. The snow flurries caused them to lose the trail and disoriented them within the mountainous landscape. He remembered seeing the worry on Jamin's face. Malcolm reminded him, "as long as we are together, we can handle anything, Brother." The peace visibly emerged on Jamin's face as Malcolm said this to him. They spent the night on the hillside where they cut pine branches to shield the open side of the large juniper they took cover under. They gathered pine needles as a barrier against the ground and to use as cover against the cold night air. They fell asleep cuddled together until the storm subsided in the morning light.

He thought again how things were different now. Malcolm was alone. He thought about Stephanie, the betrayal and hurt he felt. He thought about the government he had been so naively comforted in, that was now unraveling before his eyes. Malcolm felt truly alone--in every sense of the word. The panic inside him multiplied. He sat down on that hillside. He placed his hand over his heart and felt the quick thumping palpitate. He closed his eyes and consciously took deep and steady breaths. He let himself feel the warmth of the sun's rays on his face. He focused on the fresh air that surrounded him and filled his lungs. Malcolm's heart began to slow. He was back to the present moment…back to the peace only the wilderness had ever provided for him. Peace flowed through his body like a warm blanket covering every inch of him.

Malcolm opened his eyes and took in the scenery around him. He felt connected to this place and everything nature at the same time. He felt love…not from anyone or anything specific, yet from everything at the same time. He remembered this feeling and just sat enjoying it for 30 minutes on that hillside. He consciously thought, *if I were not afraid, if I were not alone, what would I do at this moment?*

When Malcolm was with Jamin, he was enough. He was worthwhile and important…even if it was for the pure fact that he had to be for Jamin. The abuse that Malcolm had endured as a child left deep scars, scars that reminded him that he was not worth much as the person he was. When not directly looking out for Jamin, he felt this. Malcolm remembered a moment years after coming to his parents about the abuse that had taken place. They were watching *America's Most Wanted* on the television. A young girl had been sexually abused and raped by a neighbor before fleeing the law. This criminal had raped and abused countless children within different communities he had lived in throughout the years. Malcolm's father said, "I would be in prison if that happened to my family, because I'd kill the son of a bitch."

Those words stung Malcolm to the core when he heard them. *Did he not remember? Did he not believe me?. . . or,* Malcolm thought, *"am I just not worth it?* Subconsciously, Malcolm felt he knew that the answer lay in his worth, the same lack of worth his uncle had shown him years earlier.

Malcolm again refocused on his present place, again asking the question, *If I were not afraid…if I were enough, what would I do?* He closed his eyes, felt the sun, breathed in the mountain air and made the hand sign for *I love you.* He put his hand with that sign out in front of him, for Jamin, for Stephanie, and for the mountains that helped him see so much more clearly. He brought that hand to his heart and spoke aloud. "You are enough. You are enough." Malcolm started to feel light. He felt happy, which was foreign to him in these recent times. Malcolm felt as if he was shedding pounds of baggage he had been lugging around.

Malcolm stood up and finished his trek to the summit. On top, the view around him was incredible, miles upon miles of wilderness, untouched by the society he so needed to escape. As he walked along the ridge, he saw large deer tracks with the fork in its hoof pointing outward, indicating a sizable buck. He saw game trails leading from all sides of the mountain. He followed the pair of large tracks that caught his attention to the southeast side of the ridge. He crouched low, staying near the trees to hide his outline. A human silhouetted on the top of the ridge was a sure way to cause any deer out grazing to find their way out of sight behind the foliage. He had a clear view of the ridge just east of him, as well as a ridge that teed off of the mountaintop he was on to the southwest.

Malcolm sat down near a Juniper and pulled a small pack tripod and connected his Vortex 15x50 binoculars to it. He scanned the mountainside, starting low and to his left, raising the binoculars a bit and scanning back to the right, sectioning the mountain into grids. On his sweep back to the right, he saw a three-point buck slowly grazing as it walked from left to right. It stopped as if something caught its attention. Malcolm raised his glasses in the direction the buck was looking. He saw a two-point standing above the other deer, looking in the three-point's direction. The three-point walked around a sage brush and got on the same level as this two-point. The three-point lowered its horns to signify a challenge. The two-point, significantly smaller than the three-point, took a couple of steps backwards and diverted its eyes. The three-point lifted his head in dominance as the two-point continued to back from his challenge. The three-point went back to grazing, followed by the two-point who grazed, but altered his direction slightly away from the larger buck.

Malcolm continued his grid coverage of the hill. He saw another two-point, another three-point and four doe on that hillside. Then, Malcolm stopped. Right before him was the largest buck he had ever seen in the wild. Buck generally max out at four-points on each horn. This one was atypical. From Malcolm's binoculars, he could count at least nine points on each horn. This buck was magnificent from every aspect of the word. His neck was thick and he had a good 40 pounds on the largest three-point Malcolm had spotted. Malcolm sat back from his binoculars. "Wow," he said to himself. Then put his eyes back on his binoculars to take another look and to convince himself that he was not just seeing things. It was about 4:30 in the afternoon by this time. There was only an hour or so left of daylight. Malcolm spent the next half an hour just watching this magnificent creature. At a certain point one of the three-points got near one of the doe, and just a glance from this atypical buck thwarted the advance. It was breeding season and that was his harem. This was HIS kingdom.

At a few minutes past 5:00, Malcolm slowly snuck back to the center of the ridge, out of the sight of the deer. It was too late to begin his stalk and from Malcolm's experience, his best chances were to watch them bed down in the early morning hours. Doing this would allow him to have time to figure out and plan a stalk down-wind of this buck, while he remained bedded down in the same area for the day.

Chapter 34

Malcolm's alarm went off at 5:00 the next morning. The sun would rise at 7:30, with light slowly spreading across the sky as early as 7:00 AM. He put on camouflage hunting clothes, grabbed his gear and hiked up the ridge he had climbed the previous afternoon. As he approached the ridge, he turned off his headlamp and used the light of the half-moon to direct his trek. When Malcolm came to the top of the ridge, he stopped and just listened. He could hear coyotes howling in one of the valleys below. As he slowly walked over the crest, he heard a rustling to his right. The thought of the mountain lion tracks from the day before made the hair stand up on his neck. He felt totally aware of every small sound upon that mountaintop. He inhaled the crisp cool air that filled his lungs. The smell of dirt, sage, and pine scented the air around him. He was fully present, fully alive at this moment. *This is why I love hunting so much*, he thought to himself. Nothing else brought him this level of awareness.

As he got to where he felt he may be able to see where the

rustling came from, he froze. He stood totally still for about 10 minutes. Then he saw them. A doe and her fawn were slowly grazing on some bitter bush. He could feel a slight breeze on his face, which meant he was downwind and the deer would most likely not be able to pick up his scent. The doe and fawn walked within 10 feet of Malcolm. The fawn and then the doe looked right at him. He remained frozen. After about 30 seconds, they began eating again and worked their way across the ridge and down towards where he had seen the deer the day before.

Malcolm began walking again, stopping and listening every 20 feet or so. He eventually got to the NE side of the ridge and sat back under a large juniper. This is the same mountainside that he had watched the deer the day before, but he was much further down the mountain. He was within 30 yards from where he had seen one of the three-points pass, which could give him a great shot if it followed the same path, however, the big atypical was on his mind and the one he would try to locate. After sitting for a few minutes, he grabbed the tripod from his pack and attached his binoculars. He had another 45 minutes before he could see anything beyond 30 yards, besides a potential silhouette on the ridge.

He sat back on his pack and looked at the clear night sky. The stars were unbelievably bright and the milky way was clear, stretching across the sky. Malcolm watched a shooting star streak across the sky and thought about the many stars, planets, and worlds out there beyond his own. He felt small and insignificant, but then a moment later, felt connected to everything around him and out there. The troubles that he had with Stephanie and with what was going on within the government, no longer seemed larger than life. Clarity seemed to grow within him. It was not specific, but it was comforting to not feel so alone.

The stars became more dim as the light of the approaching sun spread across the land before him. Malcolm scanned the mountainside with his binoculars. He spotted two doe feeding on the hillside. He continued to scan. As more light emerged from behind the eastern ridge, more deer came into view. Then, he saw him, big, beautiful and magnificent. The king of this ridge. The largest atypical buck Malcolm had ever seen stood just 150 yards in front of him. Malcolm watched as he prodded the doe around him. The buck looked up, smelled the air and emulated his magnificence. Something caught his attention and this buck's gaze locked onto something to the north.

Malcolm scanned with his binoculars further in that direction. There it was, a four point. Large and strong, but still not even in the same class as the atypical. The four-point continued to encroach on the atypical's turf and had his sights on a doe that had strayed a little further from the herd. The atypical started his advance and let out a snort, which got the four-point's attention. The atypical continued walking briskly towards the four-point. The four-point remained fixed on the atypical, seeming to stand his ground, hormones and continuing his line, threw caution to the side. They now stood just 20 yards apart.

Malcolm could feel the tension in the air coming from these two warriors. The atypical prodded the doe and she moved up near the others in his harem. The atypical lowered his head in challenge; the four-point did the same. They each walked slowly toward one another, the atypical a little more brisk in his approach. When five yards apart, the four-point surged, head down, horns out front towards the atypical. The atypical answered in the same manner and they locked horns with a clash. Dust kicked up and the brute strength of the atypical moved the four-point backwards.

The four-point disengaged and moved uphill from the atypical for a better vantage point. He again surged towards the atypical. They locked horns with the atypical on the downside of the mountain. His footing slipped for a moment and the four-point moved him back. Then with a fierce side thrash of the head, horns locked, the atypical threw the four-point from his feet and he rolled once down the hill. The atypical was now on higher ground. This time the atypical didn't stop, he advanced again on the four-point with his horns, hitting him before the four-point even fully got to his feet. He fell further down the hill. The atypical stood dominant above him. The four-point averted his gaze and loped away from his defeat.

Wow, Malcolm thought to himself. Never had he witnessed such a display. Over the next hour, Malcolm watched as the atypical resumed grazing on hillside shrubs. Eventually he lay down below a large juniper. The doe who had been the subject of this event, lay down near him, under a couple of juniper to the south.

Malcolm rubbed some fine dirt between his fingers and let it fall to check the breeze. It was moving softly from south to north, which meant that he would plan his approach from the north to keep his scent from the buck. He looked across the ravine and saw a light clearing of brown weeds move up the mountainside about 100 yards north from where the buck lay. About 40 yards to the north of the buck were two large boulders that he could use as land markers as he made his approach south after walking the clearing up. It was time and Malcolm slowly, cautiously, and quietly started his way 30 yards down his side of the ravine.

It took Malcolm about an hour and a half to go down 30 yards, up 150 and over another 60 yards. He walked 10-20 feet at a time, stopping, listening, and using his binoculars to scan the vegetation around him. The last thing he needed to do was to stumble upon another bedding deer that would alert the atypical to his approach.

Now he crouched right behind the boulders, just 40 yards from where he had seen the atypical from across the ridge. His heart thumped, sweat filled his brow, and his legs were shaky from the slow and cautious approach. Before hunting, he never would have imagined the effort that it takes to move silently across the land, creeping undetected. He could have run up and down that hill a couple of times and not felt the fatigue he felt now. The adrenaline amplified the shakiness of his limbs.

Slowly, he crept around the boulder. Malcolm carefully

brought his binoculars up to his eyes. He wanted to see every detail of where the buck lay, the direction he faced, and the doe around him. He spotted the buck, lying down with his head and antlers up, looking out over the valley. There were no doe that Malcolm could see between him and the buck. There were two near the buck on his south side and he spotted one other doe underneath a tree even further south, which he hadn't seen when he watched them from across the ridge. He knew there were probably more to the south, but that shouldn't matter.

Malcolm continued to move closer. After every few feet he moved, he used his binoculars to scan the area. When he got within 30 yards, he began taking things even slower. The next 6 yards took 30 minutes for him to travel. Using his rangefinder, he knew that he was just 24 yards from the buck. He wouldn't attempt to go any closer. He saw one doe near the buck stand up and start to graze. The buck remained fixed in his position. The doe started walking north towards Malcolm. Adrenaline kicked up again. Malcolm didn't want to lose his chance by being "made" by this approaching doe.

Malcolm remained totally still, except for his left arm, where he slowly grabbed an inch size rock from the ground. When he was sure the doe was not looking in his direction, he tossed the stone just 5 yards above the atypical. The atypical and the doe looked in the direction of where the rock landed. After a couple of minutes, they forgot about the sound and the atypical looked back over the valley. Malcolm tossed another rock, landing close to the same spot it had landed before. This time, the buck rose to its feet and looked in the direction of the sound. Malcolm drew his bow and held for the buck to take one more step to fully display the spot right behind his front leg, which would ensure a clean kill.

As Malcolm held, the magnificence of this animal fully began to reside within him. Beautiful, powerful, and in line with all the universe seemed to be and is. Images flooded his mind. Images of people exploiting, enslaving, and killing beauty around them for personal gain...despite what it meant to the natural order of everything. He could see the people behind the numbing of society, the elimination of feeling, and the pain inflicted on those who "would not go gentle into that good night." The poem by Dylan Thomas increased in significance within his mind. "Rage, rage, against the dying of the light!"

Malcolm lowered the tension on his bow, sat still and watched. Today, he would not do as others have done, just because he could. He would not make this ripple within the universe. Other days, may mean different acts, but this was not for today. This magnificent animal had just given Malcolm a gift. A gift of clarity. A gift of knowing what he must be true to, regardless of the paths and threats that come from others in his world outside this wilderness experience.

Malcolm watched for another 20 minutes, then crept back the way he'd come. The atypical would never know how close he came to ending, nor would he know what he had given to Malcolm, but the universe did and they were both a part of that.

Chapter 35

"At this moment, you are where you are meant to be…when you realize that, life happens" – Eckhart Tolle

Stephanie slowly opened her eyes. Her mind was still foggy from the evening and night she was waking up from. She looked around the unfamiliar room. It was still dark. The sun had not come up, but she could see early light slowly creeping into the darkness from the window inside the bedroom. She was naked and a man was next to her in bed. Stephanie searched her mind to try to uncover what had happened last night and where she had gone. She remembered drinking with her roommates before leaving for a club. She could remember dancing and drinking at the club. She also had brief images of kissing a guy in the club and right outside of the building. Stephanie looked at the person next to her. This was not the guy she had remembered kissing. He was different. She could remember smoking something in the cool air outside the club and that is where her memory stopped.

Stephanie looked across the floor for her clothes. She spotted her skirt and top and sat up. Her mind was so foggy…and she hurt from what must have been rough sex. She couldn't put an image or a memory to what had happened, but her body told her part of the story. Stephanie looked around the bed and then within the blanket for her underwear. She found it at the foot of the bed. When she picked them up, they were ripped on one side and stretched out. She threw them back on the floor and put on her skirt and top. She walked towards the bedroom door, opened it the rest of the way and walked out.

The remnant of a party covered the apartment living area. There were several people lying on the couch and the floor around the room. She could smell a faint, but pungent odor of vomit. Her shoes were near the front entrance. She slipped them on. She had had a small handbag with her phone, credit card, cash, and license in it when she left for the club that night. She couldn't see it anywhere. She saw a house phone on the corner of a kitchen counter. Stephanie picked it up and dialed her cell phone. She heard the ringing and followed it. She found her handbag on the floor next to an end-table near one of the couches. She grabbed it, left the house phone on the end-table and walked out of the condominium.

It was cool outside, but not cold, like she had expected. She was in a townhouse complex. Stephanie could hear water running from a stream beyond the trees and shrubs at the edge of the property. This unit was on the end of the complex. Still she didn't know where she was. She walked around to find the address on the unit and walked still a little farther down the front street until she saw a road sign, which read Melody. Stephanie began to cry. "Melody" was a direct contrast to what she felt of her life, her circumstances, and her worth.

Tears turned into sobs and the world around her became even more fuzzy as she looked through her water-filled eyes. After several minutes of crying, Stephanie typed the address into her phone and discovered that she was in Broomfield, which is a suburb just north of Denver. She searched taxi services on her phone and ordered one to her location. Stephanie sat down against a boulder on the edge of the property. There were several trees and some scrub oak to her right, which bordered the stream. In her mind, life was lost, her world was done. The hopes and dreams she once had were shattered into so many pieces they were no longer recognizable or viable to her.

Stephanie sobbed again with every bit of what she had left…which seemed only to be pain, disappointment, and a deep feeling of worthlessness. In the midst of Stephanie's weeping, she heard a buzzing that came from behind her and continued until it was right in front of her. She looked up and saw a hummingbird just three feet in front of her face, where it stayed, as if looking into her eyes, beating its wings. A rush of peace and warmth flowed through Stephanie. She felt a deep sense of love and of being loved. The bird, which was looking straight at Stephanie, broke that gaze and looked toward her right foot, then back to

Stephanie's face. It was as if it pointed to the tattoo on her ankle. She had never really held a tangible sense of connectedness to an individual bird before, but she felt it now, as if it were telling her what she needed to know. The hummingbird remained where it was for a moment, still looking at Stephanie, and then flew due east, directly toward the tip of the rising sun.

Another deep wave of warmth flooded Stephanie's body. She felt an aliveness growing inside, so contrary to the fog she had come to this spot with. Stephanie wept again, but this time it was different. She wept with a feeling of hope and love that seemed to embrace her. Stephanie had never felt anything like this, and it came to her in the midst of the lowest time in her life. She touched the tattoo on her ankle. Images of her sitting on her father's lap on the veranda outside her childhood home in Marysvale flooded her mind. They would sit there for hours watching hummingbirds, sometimes 10 at a time, visiting the red sugar-water hummingbird feeders they had hanging outside the veranda. While sitting there, her father told her stories and spoke to her about the things his years on earth had taught him.

Stephanie's father often told her about the Native Americans that inhabited this area before they lived there, and at other times they would hunt for the arrowheads that the Native Americans had left in the hills around their house. When Stephanie was no more than six, she remembered her father asking her one day,

"Do you know why hummingbirds are so important my

little lady?" She always felt so comfortable and safe out on her veranda upon her father's lap, watching the birds. Stephanie shook her head no.

"On cold nights, the hummingbird's heart slows down and it doesn't move. The Native Americans often believed that they died during the cold dark times of the night. As the sun starts to peak over the eastern horizon, the hummingbird's heart speeds up and comes back to life. Because of this, hummingbirds came to symbolizes a resurrection or a rebirth." Her father paused for a moment, then continued,

"There are times, sometimes very long times, that we forget who we are, where we come from, and what we are a part of. Sometimes we feel dead in a sense, but there is always a rebirth, a remembering from that part of us that never forgets. Whenever we feel bad or something has really hurt us, the hummingbird opens your heart and helps you remember."

They sat silent for a moment and just watched the birds dart to and from the bird feeders.

"Do you see the wings flapping on those hummingbirds?" Stephanie's father asked.

"Yeah, but they're kinda blurry."

Her father smiled. "The hummingbird beats its wings in the symbol of infinity, which never ends."

Stephanie's father drew a picture of the sideways 8. "You see, it never ends. It goes on forever. Just like we do. Every one of us is a part of something wonderful and nothing can ever take that away. It goes on forever. Never forget sweetheart...you are something wonderful. Do you know that?" Stephanie smiled and shook her head yes, snuggling deeper into her father's lap.

Stephanie's mind then took her to another time a couple of years later when she was eight. She was walking through the hills with her father during the early twilight hours. As the light began to rise in the east, they sat down on the hilltop and watched the sun come up. Stephanie's father spoke as the edges of the sun first began to glow over the horizon.

"The Native Americans that used to live here believe that every direction means something different. The east, where the sun comes up, means new beginnings or awakening. There are times that everyone of us must go through the dark, and it's hard to see what's around us and what it is we're supposed to do, or why we are here. In the east, we see the sun come up with warmth and light that helps us feel and see the way things really are...all the beautiful things that are around us...and that are a part of us. We can see things that we couldn't see when it was night."

Stephanie's father looked down at her. She looked back and up into his eyes. She could still see every detail in his face within her memory. Now looking into her eyes he said, "Every time the sun comes up, look for something you didn't see before. If you look to see something new, something beautiful, you will always find it."

Stephanie traced the tattoo on her right ankle with her finger. It was a round compass with N, W, S, and E for each direction. In the middle of the compass was a hummingbird with a blue and green body flying due east.

Stephanie saw the yellow taxi pull into the grounds of the town homes. She got up, flagged the driver over and got inside.

Chapter 36

Malcolm walked up the stairs to his apartment with his hands full of his camping and hunting gear. As he did, he felt anxiety grow slightly within him. He distinctly thought about how easy it was to lose the clarity of the presence he had just felt. It was as if he walked back into the artificial matrix he had left just days before. He set his sleeping bag down and tried to turn the knob. It was locked, which gave Malcolm a small sense of relief. A locked door meant that there was probably not someone unexpected inside. He unlocked the door and walked in towards his room. When he pushed his room door open, he stopped. Someone was lying in his bed. "Malcolm," he heard a voice say. At first he felt comfort, relief, and such a strong longing for that voice. As he walked to the bedside, hurt, jealousy, and anger flowed through him. Malcolm took a step back and sat on the floor with his back leaning against the wall.

"Malcolm," Stephanie said. "I am so sorry. I am so sorry for what I've done to you."

Malcolm had wanted to hear these words so badly, but hurt and anger continued to fill his thoughts. When he saw her, he saw other men that didn't care for Stephanie the way he did, probably doing things with her that they had never done. She got up from the bed and sat by Malcolm on the floor. Stephanie put her hand across his stomach and laid her head against his shoulder.

"I don't expect you to forgive me. I know that I've hurt you. I'm sorry."

Tears began to flow down Malcolm's face. He sat on the floor with his body and arms limp...his core defeated. Stephanie reached up and wiped the tears from each side of his face.

"What are you thinking?" Malcolm would not look Stephanie in the face, and he just shook his head.

"I understand if you can't forgive me. I don't know if I can really forgive me," Stephanie said looking into his face and turning his towards her. "I love you Malcolm."

Malcolm's tears began to flow again and turned into sobs. Stephanie sat up and pulled him to her, putting his head on her chest. Malcolm relented, continuing to sob, while Stephanie held him.

"I couldn't take what is going on," she said. "...and I fell apart. I ran away from everything I care about." She paused for a moment, then said, "come on."

Stephanie started to get up, Malcolm leaned back and looked at the hand that she extended him. "Come on."

Malcolm took her hand, stood up and they both lay down

on the bed together, this time with Stephanie lying on his chest. He put his arm around her and they lay silent for a while, until sleep eventually found both of them.

After several hours Stephanie woke to see Malcolm staring forward towards the wall in front of his bed.

"What are you thinking?" she asked.

"We have to finish this. Regardless of what happens with us, we need to finish what we started."

"Okay," Stephanie answered, as she lay her head back on his chest. Malcolm tickled her back as they lay there.

"Do you think you'll ever be able to forgive me?" Stephanie said breaking the silence.

"I love you. That's why it hurts so bad... but, regardless of what we do, what's going on is bigger than us. Let's just take things as they go."

"I'll make it up to you Malcolm. I'm never going to hurt you like this again. I love you. I'm sorry."

Stephanie didn't tell him about the rape and what it did to her psychologically. She didn't fully understand it herself. She still blamed herself for putting herself in that situation and for all that happened after.

Chapter 37

The next day Stephanie and Malcolm met with Professor Walker. Malcolm filled both of them in on what he and Professor Temkin had found out, including the 4 F's utilized to gain control over the masses.

"You have done an amazing job. Religion was one of my earlier theories that I've looked into, but I had no idea about how deep the government was into this conspiracy until after you two started working on this project." Professor Walker looked both Malcolm and Stephanie in the eyes. "I'm sorry for what I got you into."

"This is something that has to be done Professor," said Malcolm. "It impacts everyone. It takes everyone's life a little at a time." After a brief pause, Malcolm continued,

"Tell us why you felt religion was such a significant part of the numbing of society."

"For centuries religion has been a primary tool for those that want to promote a culture of separateness and isolationism by promoting that my beliefs and my religion are superior to those of others. Religious leaders also brew up non-acceptance and even hate against societal subgroups. This includes other ethnicities, like the mark of Cain for those of African heritage, which allowed many Christian believers to make peace with the enslavement of blacks during our early American history. Hitler also used this strategy with the planned annihilation of Jews.

Even without direction to avoid interaction with 'outsiders,' at almost a subconscious level, people avoid deep conversations and relationships with those that are not a part of their specific group. This allows the dehumanization of others. If they aren't seen as real people, they don't require the same rights and respect as those who are a part of what the group considers to be mainstream. The majority of wars throughout history and even now are fueled by religion. Those who hold the power of the religion, often hold the power of the people. It reaches even further than nationalism, which can also be a strong tool. But, with religion, it holds the power of God, or what those claim to be the word of God to carry blessings or consequences well beyond this life."

"So basically, it does naturally what the chemicals do artificially," Malcolm said.

"Exactly," confirmed Professor Walker. "That's why you see so much power with religious institutions here in the United

States, with very strong financial incentives in the form of their tax-exempt status. This financial benefit occurs despite malls and other money-making ventures that are started by these groups that have nothing to do with religion."

"However," continued Professor Walker, "now we see a slow falling away from religion within some groups. To compensate, other forms of lulling are also gaining traction. You see an escape from reality, a kind of artificial reality being created within a larger population with things like drugs. We now have the legalization of marijuana in several states. Other tools like social media have taken hold and are even expanded through government internet and phone programs. But, even without these tools, excessive activity in general can have the same impact. Whenever one's mind is so full of external stimuli, it covers over what is actually deep and true within one's self. Now couple that with chemicals that further numb the people, and those in charge can basically take control of what they want.

But, going back to religion, the tools that are most impactful are the ones that also fill another innate need. The need to connect to others. That is why religion is so powerful and those in control are so focused on continuing that avenue. Whether or not the specific culture is healthy or unhealthy, that connection with another person or a group, and acceptance by that group, will move people to do things they would have never done on their own."

"So, what do we do knowing this?" asked Stephanie.

"I'm glad you asked. The Office of Religion and Global Affairs is conducting a meeting of religious leaders next week in Denver. The major Christian, Jewish, and Muslim US leaders have all been invited to attend. This might be a good place to gain more insight into what direction is pushed towards these religious leaders. I know for a fact that the representative of the Archdiocese of Denver will not be in attendance. He was called to meet with the Pope in Rome. This might be a way in."

"How can you use that to get in?" asked Stephanie.

"People are bound to know what the Archbishop looks like, but I could pose as the secretary of the archdiocese to try to obtain access. Not only is he much less recognizable, but those in that position can change."

"What about us?" asked Malcolm.

"This is a perfect opportunity for you to put on your best reporter faces and try to get in as a representative of the media." Both Malcolm and Stephanie nodded their heads in agreement.

"Okay, let's do it," confirmed Professor Walker.

Chapter 38

Tuesday of the following week, Malcolm, Stephanie, and Professor Walker went to the conference center in downtown Denver where the Office of Religion and Global Affairs would facilitate the meeting. As the secretary of the archdiocese, Professor Walker didn't need to find traditional religious garb. A suit would work fine for an occasion like this. At the entrance, the reservation for each person that entered the conference center was checked. Professor Walker identified himself as, Damian Demarco, secretary to the archbishop.

"I'm sorry Mr. Demarco. I don't have you on the list," said the young man at the front desk.

"I am representing the office of the Archdiocese of Denver and I'm attending per the Archbishop's request."

The young man again looked through the list of attendees and said, "Give me one moment, and I'll go work on straightening this out." He stood up, walked a few steps away from the table and dialed someone on his mobile phone.

Two minutes later a man in a suit walked up to the front desk.

"Mr. Demarco, thank you for representing the Archdiocese in this important meeting," he said while extending his hand. Professor Walker shook the hand, saying,

"You are most welcome."

"Please come in," the man in the suit told him.

Chapter 39

Professor Temkin traveled to Palo Alto, CA to the home of his previous director at Stanford. Michael Wilcox was a scientist that obtained the position just two years after Edward Temkin had joined the research and development team there. Michael Wilcox had moved up the ranks and established credibility with Washington through his work within the National Institute of Health (NIH). His predecessor at Stanford, John Woodward, practically disappeared one day. An email was sent from him to all within the department, notifying every one of his resignation to "pursue other personal interests and obligations." He informed the group that Michael Wilcox, Ph.D. would take over as Director.

Professor Temkin remembered thinking the quick and almost seamless transition to this change in leadership seemed odd. He had not received any inclination of Professor Woodward's imminent departure, nor had he heard any rumblings around active recruitment nor additional personnel to be added to the department.

After Professor Woodward's departure, he learned from one of John's close friends that his wife had been diagnosed with a rare form of cancer the months preceding his departure. Learning that Professor Woodward's days with his wife may be quickly numbered helped Professor Temkin understand the departure, in a sense.

In the months after his departure, Professor Temkin learned from the same individual that John's wife had begun an experimental drug treatment for her cancer, which put the condition into remission. What Professor Temkin didn't know now, but would find out later, directly from John Woodward, is that after learning of his wife's diagnosis and poor prognosis, an individual had approached him. This individual had said,

"My employer knows of your wife's condition and prognosis. He has access to a treatment not yet approved for this condition that has been shown to cure her type of cancer. My employer is well connected with many resources and is willing to take care of your wife's treatment. He is also willing to ensure that money will not be an issue for your family."

John Woodward had burst out in tears when he listened to the words this man said.

"However, there is one condition," this man had told Professor Woodward after a pause. "You are to resign as Director of your program at Stanford."

John resigned, treatment began, and money, equal to what he had been paid for his position at Stanford, was anonymously deposited into his checking account monthly. John never found out who was behind what had been done. He was just thankful to have a new outlook on life with the prospect of many more years with his wife.

When Michael Wilcox joined, he doubled the research team, bringing in people that had worked for him previously at the NIH. Dr. Wilcox was the most vocal in working to debunk and discredit the findings and publications that Professor Temkin put out to educate the medical community and public around the potential risks of the vaccine they had developed.

Professor Temkin knew that Michael Wilcox was entrenched with those behind what was occurring. His hope was that somehow he could obtain tangible proof of the conspiracy. Over the next several days, Professor Temkin watched the house of Michael Wilcox. Dr. Wilcox lived in the house with his wife Sariah. They had two grown sons that lived nearby within the Northern California bay area. Each morning during the week, Dr. Wilcox left the house at 6:00 AM. Several hours later, between 9:00 and 9:15 AM, Sariah had two girlfriends that would stop by the house, and the three women would walk between an hour and an hour and 15 minutes. Sariah left through the garage and typed a code on the keypad outside of the garage door to get back in when she returned. The afternoon was unpredictable. Sometimes Sariah would stay at the house. Other times Professor Temkin would see the garage open and Sariah would pull out in her Mercedes Sports Coupe. Sometimes she would be gone for 30-40 minutes. Other times she would arrive home just before her husband did at 6:00 PM.

There was an alarm system on the house, but from what Professor Temkin could tell, the alarm didn't seem to be set during Sariah's morning walks with her girlfriends. On the third day of observation, Professor Temkin made his move. Through binoculars he had watched Sariah punch the code on the garage keypad several times. As she had punched the code, her finger went straight down the middle of the keypad and up one or two numbers, still in the middle row. After Sariah walked out of sight with her friends, he punched in the numbers "2-5-8-0-8 enter." Nothing happened. He tried another sequence. Maybe the code just went straight down . . . "2-5-8-0 enter." Still nothing happened. Professor Temkin felt the adrenaline well up inside. He looked around and couldn't see anybody watching. He tried another sequence, "2-5-8-0-5 enter." Still nothing happened. He closed his eyes to visualize her pressing the keys, counting the key punches in his mind. It was four. Four punches. He punched "2-5-8-5 enter." The garage began to open.

Once the garage door was open enough for him to walk through, he slipped inside. There was Sariah's Mercedes Sports Coupe and the empty space where Michael Wilcox parked his silver Jaguar F-Type convertible. Professor Temkin pressed the garage door button that was located near the door leading into the house. The garage door closed and Professor Temkin opened the door to the inside.

The interior of the house was immaculate. The first door he walked through lead into a type of "mud-room," but there was not a speck of mud in it. On the wall were several hooks with jackets and hats. There was a small wash basin and a water fountain. When he walked through the mud-room, it opened up into an open layout with large walnut French doors to his left at the front of the house and a formal sitting area just beyond that. To his right, was a kitchen and dining area with top-end craftsmanship, including travertine floors, large marble countertops and walnut cabinet doors. To the right of the kitchen was a family room with a leather sofa, love seat and flat screen TV. Even further to his right was a hallway. He quickly walked down it.

At the end of the hallway there were two doors, one on the right side of the hallway, towards the garage, and one on his left, towards the back of the house. He first looked to his left where the door was still ajar. As he peered into the room, he could see that it was their bedroom with large glass French doors leading to the back yard. Professor Temkin then tried the other door. It was locked. He walked into the bedroom area and looked on the dresser and bedside area for a place where a key might be kept. On the top of the dresser was a large flat box that had some of Sariah's jewelry, bracelets and watches inside. Inside the drawers were clothes. Professor Temkin felt around the edges of the drawers, but found nothing. He walked over to the bedside table and looked inside the drawers. Inside the top drawer on what he figured to be Michael's side was a beautiful Kimber 45 acp handgun. The anxiety Professor Temkin felt inside grew even further. He looked more and still found nothing that would help him open the locked door.

Professor Temkin left the bedroom, careful to leave things as they had been when he entered, and stood before the locked door. That's when he heard a terrifying sound. It was the garage door opening. He had to think of something quickly. He took his wallet from his back pocket and grabbed a credit card. He worked to slide it into the door jamb. The credit card was too thick. He pulled out his license and tried that. It was more flexible and was able to be worked into the door jamb where the door latched. He heard the door that led into the house open and Sariah saying goodbye to her friends, followed by the noise of the garage closing. With his license in place, he simultaneously pushed his license into the latch, while pulling back on the door. The latch recessed into the door and quickly, yet quietly, he opened the door just enough for him to slip inside. Once inside, Professor Temkin slowly and quietly closed the door. He turned on the doorknob to ensure that it was still locked and just stood silent on the inside of Michael Wilcox's study.

"Is somebody there?" he heard Sariah say. There was a pause, then a "hello." Professor Temkin heard footsteps leading up the hall. The doorknob to the study jiggled as Sariah tried to turn it from the hallway. Professor Temkin stood still looking at the doorknob, practically holding his breath. He heard her walk away towards what he assumed was her bedroom. He looked around the study. There were three large windows, two towards the front of the house and one towards the north side with closed blinds on all three windows. In the corner was a large wooden desk with a computer screen and keyboard on top of it. The desk faced out towards the front of the house. There were short file cabinets on the north wall. On the south wall were bookshelves and a large safe with a dial combination on it.

As Professor Temkin continued to stand still, he heard Sariah walk out of the bedroom towards him. Still, he hardly breathed and searched his mind in a panic around what to do if she opened that study door. The footsteps walking towards him continued to go past the study door and proceeded down the hall towards the kitchen and family room area. A moment later, he could hear the muffled sound of the TV. A brief sense of relief came over him. He crept over to the safe, careful not to make a sound. The travertine floor had a large Persian rug covering the majority of it in this room, which made keeping quiet fairly easy.

Professor Temkin positioned himself in front of the safe and pulled a piece of paper out of his pocket. He had written several potential combinations with significant dates in Michael Wilcox's life, which included birthdate, wife's birthdate, wedding date, college graduation, Ph.D. date, children's birthdates, and tried them one by one. Nothing worked. After 30 minutes of trying everything he could think of, he sat down on the floor with his back against the safe. He wasn't going to get in today and he needed to find a way out of the house before Michael came home at 6:00. It was 11:45 now, so he had time. Professor Temkin had the impression that this study was purely Michael's and that it would be very unlikely for Sariah to enter without him being home. Professor Temkin sat by the safe for another hour, his eyes getting heavy. Eventually, he dozed off.

At 2:00 PM, Professor Temkin opened his eyes. He had been dreaming about the work he had done with the institution and Michael Wilcox. "Belief, Separation, Submission, Control," was a concept he had overheard Michael talking about on the phone one day when he worked at the University with him. It had stood out to him because it corresponded with another sequence of letters that were header's on the project they were working on, "BSSC." Professor Temkin counted out the positional number each of the letters had in the alphabet. B is the second letter in the alphabet, S is the 19th letter in the alphabet, and C is the third letter in the alphabet. He stood up, dialed 2-19-19-3 onto the safe dial and tried to turn the latch. It opened.

Chapter 40

Once inside, Mark tried as much as he could to avoid others, but despite his best efforts, leaders from various religious organizations came up to introduce themselves and to inquire about who he represented. One man in particular, a local delegate for the Methodist church approached saying,

"Hello, I hear that you are here representing the archdiocese? It is a pleasure to make your acquaintance. The archbishop and I are close friends. I didn't know that he was going to be able to send a delegate to the conference."

"It is a pleasure to meet you as well," Mark replied. "Yes, he wanted to ensure we were represented." Mark then tried to politely move on, but the Methodist delegate continued.

"How long have you worked with the archbishop?"

"It hasn't been too terribly long, but at the same time, it seems like forever," Mark answered and offered a polite smile. The Methodist delegate smiled back.

"How is his sister Gloria doing?"

"She is doing well, I'll ensure she receives your regards."

"Please do," the delegate said, still smiling and they parted ways.

A small man hitting a chime began to walk through the lobby, signifying that it was close to starting time and for those in the corridor to begin moving towards the auditorium. While on his way, he saw several state senators in attendance that he recognized. Mark then felt someone grab the back of his left arm. Immediately after he felt the pressure on his left arm, someone grabbed Mark's right arm. Mark looked to both of his sides. They were stocky men in suits, each with an earpiece.

"Can I help you?" Mark asked.

"We need you to come with us for a moment."

"Is there a problem?"

"Please come with us sir," one of the men stated.

As Mark Walker was escorted back towards where he had come in, everything came together when he saw the face of the Methodist delegate. He looked at Mark.

"Sir, I don't know who you are, but I do know the sister of the archbishop well, and her name is not Gloria."

Chapter 41

Ten minutes after Mark had entered the conference, Malcolm and Stephanie tried to look as "press-like" as they could, including a notepad, pen and "press" tag around their neck. They walked to the entrance and were immediately shut down. "The press is not allowed at this function," said the person at the front entrance. Malcolm tried to protest, but two men quickly stepped forward and helped to usher them away.

Malcolm and Stephanie continued walking away from the conference center toward a park across the street. On the way, they stopped by a coffee stand and Malcolm ordered two cups of coffee for them. With coffee in hand, they walked over to a park bench and sat down.

"There is no way we can stop this Malcolm. It's too big," commented Stephanie. They sat in silence for a minute.

"There is always a way. We just need to figure out what that is," replied Malcolm.

"Just because you say it, doesn't make it true, Malcolm. I was blind to what the world was, not because it used to be better, but because I didn't see the way things really are."

"It's just that a few people in big positions have gotten control. We need to stop them before it's too late."

"It's not just these people, it's all people. I used to believe in others, but the more I learn, the more I see. From people who lead community church congregations and molest kids, to parents who ignore the needs of their children to fulfill their own primal urges, to the 'upstanding citizen' who takes something of value someone accidentally left on a park bench…thinking, if I don't take it, someone else will."

"So it's up to us, the last two, to make a difference," Malcolm said as he winked at Stephanie.

"I'm just like all of the others, escaping, fulfilling primal urges, hurting others. This place isn't good. People aren't good," Stephanie said.

Malcolm sat quietly after Stephanie finished speaking. After a minute, he spoke, "Follow your Bliss and the Universe will open doors where there were only walls."

"Did you just make that up?" Asked Stephanie.

"It's a quote by Joseph Campbell. It was true years ago and it is true now."

"I think that's wishful thinking, but I hope you're right."

Again, Malcolm and Stephanie sat silent, just watching the people around them and thinking about their situation.

"Well, hopefully Professor Walker can have some luck," Malcolm finally said, breaking the silence. Stephanie continued to sit quietly, sipping her coffee. "I promised that I would go see Rajan and Ryan. The least I can do is try to make a part of their day a little better for them."

"You don't think you've done enough?" asked Stephanie.

"What do you mean?" asked Malcolm.

"You're the reason they're going to foster care. You're no different than me or any of the others."

"Do you think their life was good before their mother was killed?"

"That's my point Malcolm. The world is not a good place...and when we get involved, nothing gets better."

"I'm going to go see those kids. They're temporarily with an aunt 20 minutes from here."

"They're in Colorado? How convenient," Stephanie said annoyed at the thought of continuing to get involved in things that shouldn't pertain to them.

"Things happen for a reason Stephanie." Malcolm managed a weak smile. "I would like you to come, but it's up to you." Malcolm stood up and started walking towards his car. Stephanie continued to sit on the bench. Malcolm stopped and turned towards Stephanie. "Will you come with me Steph? Please?" Stephanie stood up and walked with Malcolm to the car.

Chapter 42

When Professor Temkin opened the safe, he found a cigar box full of cash and a stack of folders with documents in them. On the outside of one accordion envelope, *BSSC* was written. With Sariah still in the house, and with Michael Wilcox not expected to arrive back home for another four hours, he decided to see what was within the documents he now held in his hands. His anxiety about being caught by Mrs. Wilcox had tempered significantly. The longer Professor Temkin spent in the office, the more confident he was with his impression that this was Michael's office, his domain and that Sariah probably didn't even have a key.

What he noticed first was a section that contained his own work, identifying the emotional lulling that the flu vaccine caused with subjects that it had been administered to. What intrigued him even further was that there were research documents dated years before his publication documenting a similar compound that had caused apathy within rats and then within human subjects.

Unfortunately, this chemical also caused premature death, resulting from physical atrophy that impacted both the body and especially the brain of rats, pigs, and dogs.

Slight variations of the chemical were studied in combination with flu vaccines, fluoride, pesticides, and narcotics. During the time that Professor Temkin had been working at Stanford and began making the connection with the "undesirable" side-effects of the flu vaccine, he was totally unaware of concurrent research looking at bonding this chemical structure to other compounds. What was unique about the component that caused apathy is that it was not a separate chemical compound added to vaccines, fluoride, pesticides, and narcotics. It actually consisted of a specific chemical chain that was added to these other compounds, making it one molecule with a common "apathy" chain. What this did was make it difficult for researchers, like himself, to identify the pirate chemical, due to the fact that it was a distinct part of the parent molecule.

A different subfolder was labeled "Drug War." Documents within this section originated back in the 1930s and documented some of the past work conducted by Harry Anslinger, the first commissioner of the Federal Bureau of Narcotics. Harry Anslinger gained notoriety by saving the railroad that he worked for $50,000 by investigating a claim and providing proof of fraudulence. From 1917-1928, Anslinger worked with military and police organizations throughout the world, with a focus on stopping international drug trafficking. He was fueled by the haunting wails of his mother suffering from narcotic withdrawal when he was a child. He was 12 years old when he witnessed this happening to his mother. He knew that something terrible had possessed her. What exactly that was at the time, he didn't know. His father urgently directed him to saddle up a horse and to ride into town to pick up a package from the pharmacy. "I never forgot those screams," he wrote years later as an adult.

This background and experience made Harry Anslinger the perfect messenger to embark on the first Separation, Submission, and Control (SSC) initiative. Belief was not added to the movement until a few years later. Anslinger is most famous for his war on drugs within the United States, which also resulted in similar policies throughout Europe. The drug epidemic was something that impacted all races and socioeconomic classes, however the "war" was primarily waged on the undesirables within society, particularly minorities (blacks and Hispanics) and poor whites. Specific documentation was cited around the subtle Jazz rebellion, which was an expression within the black community that also found its way into traditional middle-class America.

Billie Holiday became a face of this rebellious sub-culture. Copies of notes from Harry Anslinger himself were documented here stating, "criminalizing and eliminating those advancing the drug and anti-society subculture, most notable Billie Holiday and close associates, will squelch the movement most threatening to the Judeo-Christian standards that have made America great." After 20 years of targeting Billie Holiday, Anslinger put her under arrest and under police guard for drug possession, when she was hospitalized for cirrhosis of the liver. He prevented any of her friends and associates from seeing her. Her heroin withdrawal exacerbated the complications of liver failure. Her friends were eventually allowed in, but not soon enough to prevent her death.

By prosecuting and alienating these sub-cultures, their impact on policies and those elected to lead were better controlled, which allowed the elite to rule over the masses, instigating a class system, despite the declaration that "all men are created equal." While the drug-war continued, other tactics were being explored through legalization, which allowed another potential avenue to add the same apathy chain to widely used and now regulated substances. The first trial with legalization was with marijuana, which in itself provides a natural apathy or withdrawal from activities that could get in the way of those seeking control. It was the perfect place to start.

More and more details were discussed around different initiatives, including housing projects and abortion clinics within the communities of the "undesirables," contributing to the same outcome that the selective drug war provided. Sun Tzu and the *Art of War* were quoted on numerous occasions within the documents Professor Temkin read, "If his forces are united, separate them. If sovereign and subject are in accord, put division between them. To fight and conquer in all your battles is not supreme excellence; supreme excellence consists in breaking the enemy's resistance without fighting."

The addition of Belief to the BSSC acronym played well into these concepts. Religion soon became one of the most powerful tools by leveraging the "Word of God" to control and submit large groups of people. Government furthered this initiative through tax subsidies and backroom deals. But even without any backroom deals, the separation many of the growing religious sects produced, established one of the key tactics in control. It created a separation amongst the people. The majority of religions hold tight to very similar concepts. Only between 10% and 20% of beliefs differ among religions, but that is what those belonging to each sect focus on. That is how pastors, bishops, priests, and other religious leaders retain their loyal followership and continue the flow of tithing and offerings coming in. When specific sects went rogue, they became a focus of government elimination. They lost their tax loopholes and were labeled extremists. In many situations, the activities that these rogue religious groups were accused of doing, never occurred.

Professor Temkin spent the next hour reading through the documents within the safe. When he heard the TV turned up in the family room, Professor Temkin made copies of the sections of the folder that he felt were the most damning for those behind the conspiracy. At about 4:00 PM, he heard the sound of the TV turn off. He was in the middle of copying a section. The professor pushed pause on the copier. He heard footsteps outside the office door. They sounded as if they went into the bedroom, then back out into the main section of the house. He then heard the sound of the garage door opening. "This is it," professor Temkin thought to himself. "This is my way out." He listened intently for silence in the house and for a car to pull away. That didn't happen. Instead he heard the sound of a vehicle pulling into the garage. Professor Temkin grabbed the copies from the copy machine, put the other documents in the safe and listened intently.

He heard Mr. and Mrs. Wilcox's muffled voices coming from the great room. Professor Temkin's heart raced. He heard the heavier footsteps of who he presumed to be Michael coming down the hallway. The professor looked around the room in a panic. He needed somewhere to hide but couldn't find a good place. He may be able to get out of initial sight from someone standing at the door, but once someone entered the room, he would be exposed. He grabbed a bookend from a shelf and stood on the backside of the door. As the footsteps approached closer, it sounded like two sets of footsteps. He heard the voices more clearly now. One was Mrs. Wilcox, but the man's voice was not Michael.

They stopped right in front of the office door, which was also right in front of the master bedroom door. There was laughter and flirtatious taunting of one another. He heard the slam of the bedroom door. Five minutes later, he heard Sariah moaning. There was not going to be a better time for Professor Temkin to leave. He slowly opened the study door, with the copies of documents in hand, and walked as quietly as he could down the hallway. Professor Temkin walked to the front door and looked out the side window. Nobody was outside. He unlocked the front door, put his hand on the doorknob and stopped. A thought ran through his head. He was going to take this opportunity to inflict some marital discourse on the man who ruined his. He took his hand off of the doorknob and turned towards the alarm system panel in the entry way. He held the fire alert button down, until the alarm began to sound. He then fled through the front door, shutting it on the way out.

Chapter 43

Twenty minutes after being confronted for impersonation of a religious delegate, Mark Walker was contained by two police officers and put under arrest for impersonation to unlawfully enter a closed government meeting. After handcuffing him and reading Mark the Miranda rights, they put him in the back of a police cruiser and drove a short distance to the downtown Denver Police Station. It was a fairly large tan brick building with the jail attached. Mark looked out of place as he stepped out of the police cruiser, which attracted onlookers. The police officers walked him through the front entrance and around a corner to booking. Additional police staff took fingerprints and captured his mugshot. Mark was then escorted into a temporary cell, which held three additional inmates. They looked as if they most likely were in for drugs or theft. None of them had much size to them, so he doubted they were in for assault, which eased Mark's mind a bit.

Just before they shut the cell door, he asked the officers for his phone call. "When your time comes, I'll let you know," said the overweight officer that lead him in. This officer sat behind a small desk at the beginning of the entryway to the holding cells. The area Mark was in appeared to house a total of 6 cells, most of which held inmates in transition, before getting out or moving to a more permanent area.

Five minutes later, Mark heard the officer that brought him in bellow, "Mark Walker, you have visitors." Mark looked up to see two men in suits. A chill ran down his spine. They took him to a small room, near the cells, but separate from the main hallway. Inside the room was a table and three chairs. They asked him to take a seat and motioned to the side with a single chair. Mark took a seat, his wrists handcuffed in front. One man who stood before him was a mid-sized black man, the other was a taller white man. Both were well built and athletic looking.

"I am Special Agent Truman Sikes," said the white agent. "This is my partner, Special Agent Jeremiah Watson," he said gesturing to the agent sitting beside him.

"Are you with the FBI?" Mark asked. They both nodded their head.

"What were you doing at the conference center?" asked Agent Sikes.

"I was trying to learn about the secular sciences within the United States."

"And why were you trying to learn that, Mr. Walker?" asked Agent Watson.

"Professor Walker," Mark corrected. "I teach Sociology at the University of Denver. Religion and theology have a significant impact on behavior and the way our society interacts as a whole."

"What were you really trying to do Professor Walker?" asked Agent Watson.

"I told you what I was doing."

"We can do this the easy way or the hard way, Professor Walker. We will give you one more opportunity to do this the easy way. We know that you were not there to just do research for your curriculum."

"I told you what I was doing. That's it. I would like to speak to a lawyer."

"In federal cases like this, where acts of terrorism are suspected, you are not allowed to speak to a lawyer," answered Agent Sikes. Agent Watson stood up and motioned for the officer to take Mark back to his cell.

Chapter 44

Malcolm and Stephanie pulled up outside of Miss Rachel Aims' duplex apartment. It was in a low-income neighborhood, right next to a train track. The neighborhood and the duplex were old, with the dull brown paint on the duplex peeling off. They walked up the worn wooden steps that lead to the small porch, and Malcolm knocked on the door. Rajan opened the door. A big smile emerged on his face as he flung open the screen door and gave Malcolm a hug.

"Hey buddy. How are you doing?" asked Malcolm.

"Great!" exclaimed the young boy.

"This is my friend Stephanie," Malcolm said motioning over to her.

"It's a pleasure to meet you," Rajan said extending a hand, still smiling ear-to-ear.

"It's a pleasure to meet you, Rajan," Stephanie answered back, taking the boy's small hand in hers.

"Is Miss Aims here?" asked Malcolm.

"No, she's out," answered Rajan.

"When will she be back?" Malcolm asked.

"I don't know. She left last night with a guy."

"You've been home by yourself all night?" asked Stephanie.

"Yeah, but it's okay. I made Ryan and me some cereal." Rajan hugged Malcolm again.

"Does Miss Aims leave you home alone a lot?" asked Malcolm.

"Sometimes, but it's okay. I can take care of Ryan, plus we have a place to stay every night. We didn't always have somewhere to stay before. Come in." Malcolm and Stephanie walked inside. Ryan was watching TV.

"Hey Ryan. How're you doing?"

"I miss my mom. She's dead," Ryan said. Stephanie's heart sunk to the bottom of her gut. Rajan went over and sat by Ryan.

"It's time to turn off the TV. You've already watched an hour." Rajan turned the TV off and spoke directly to Ryan.

"I miss mom, too, Ryan. She's in a better place now where nobody can hurt her. She told me that she is looking over us every day."

"How did she tell you that if she's dead?" Ryan asked.

"She told me in a dream. When you die, your body dies, but who you are keeps living. We'll get to see her again."

Stephanie and Malcolm watched this interaction quietly. Neither could believe the depth of maturity this 6-year-old boy had. He was an old soul. Both Malcolm and Stephanie could sense it.

"We brought you a game," said Malcolm, as he pulled the game Sorry out of a large plastic bag.

"Thank you so much! We used to have Sorry but it got left somewhere we stayed. Let's play!" exclaimed Rajan excitedly. Together they set up the board, and began playing. During the game, Ryan's piece was kicked back to the beginning and Ryan began to pout and complain.

"That always happens! I always lose!"

"You haven't lost yet. You're still playing. That happened to me 6 times one game and I won. If you believe, it can happen, Ryan…it can happen." Rajan then looked at Stephanie and Malcolm for support. "Huh? It doesn't matter what happens, you can still win, right?" Rajan said looking Malcolm and Stephanie in the eyes and smiling.

"That's right." Stephanie said smiling back at the kids. Courageous optimism just exuded from Rajan, unlike anything Stephanie had seen. After a while of playing, Ryan got her last piece back home.

"See! You did it Ryan! You won! I told you. It doesn't matter what happens, you CAN STILL WIN!"

"Nice job, Ryan!" said both Malcolm and Stephanie simultaneously. Ryan smiled ear-to-ear for the first time during their visit.

Three hours later, Miss Aims came home. She looked worn from the night and scolded Rajan for letting strangers into the house. She tried to make up some excuse for being gone, but her short skirt, wrinkled blouse and the alcohol on her breath told a different story. Malcolm and Stephanie said their goodbyes to the kids.

"When will you see us again?" asked Rajan.

"Soon," answered Malcolm and they walked out the door and down the porch steps. On their way to the car, a lone rosebush caught Stephanie's attention. What grass there was amongst the dirt yard, was brown. Everything was dead or worn, and yet, right in the middle of this, flourished a lone beautiful rosebush with deep red blossoming flowers.

That visit had had an extreme impact on Stephanie. She saw this young boy that the rest of the world would pity for having such a difficult life, totally cast out that notion and actually choose his reality and his fate. *There was good in the world. One just had to acknowledge it,* she thought to herself.

Chapter 45

A few minutes after Professor Walker was escorted back to his cell, three new inmates were brought in. All three were Hispanic, well built with tattoos running down their arms, lower legs and neck. One inmate had two teardrop tattoos coming from his left eye.

"Que pasa? You looking at me?" One of the three said to Professor Walker. Mark just looked down. "That cabron was looking at me," he said to the man with teardrops.

"He was looking at you?" the man with teardrops said. They all three stood up. "This cabron was looking at you?" the man with teardrops said again with even more emphasis on the words. The third man now chimed in,

"You want his ass gringo?"

"I'm not looking for trouble," Professor Walker replied.

Ten minutes later, the professor woke up, lying on the concrete floor. His head was pounding and his blood was smeared on the cement ground around his head. He heard laughing. It started out as an echoing dream-like sound, then sharpened into reality. As Professor Walker tried to get up, pains in his sides sharpened and the thudding in his head deepened. He winced with pain. "What…you don't want his ass any more joto?" one of the men said. They all laughed deep belly laughs.

Two officers came to the cell door and asked the inmates to turn around and face the back wall. Once the other inmates complied, the two officers helped Professor Walker to his feet and escorted him back into the room where Agents Sikes and Watson were waiting.

"We figured that having alone time in your cell may help you better remember why you were at the conference," stated Agent Sikes. "Were we right?"

"Fuck you!" replied Professor Walker.

Agent Watson came back with, "We'll give you a little more time to think about it in your cell." Agent Sikes stood up and motioned for the officers to escort him back to the cell. As they grabbed the professor, he said, "wait."

"Do you remember something, Mr. Walker," asked Agent Sikes.

"Yes."

"Let him go," said Agent Watson, "What is it?"

"Suck my dick you fucking pricks."

Agent Watson shook his head, obviously surprised and irritated. "Put him back in the cell." Once back in the cell, the first few minutes after the guards left felt like hours. The beatings had resumed, again followed by everything going black, as he laid unconscious on the concrete floor.

Chapter 46

Professor Walker woke up the next afternoon in a familiar location. It was Saint John's Hospital. Malcolm, Stephanie, and Professor Temkin were all there.

"Hey, how are you feeling?" asked Stephanie.

"Like I've been beaten, run over, and killed." Professor Walker said, while managing a weak smile. "How are you?"

"Better than that," Stephanie answered.

"How was the meeting?" Malcolm asked with a smirk on his face. Professor Walker extended his middle finger over the tubes and lines that ran into his arms. They all laughed, including Professor Walker, which ended with him wincing in pain.

"I'm sorry," Malcolm said. "This is bullshit, but we've got something."

"What?" asked Professor Walker. Malcolm and Stephanie both looked at Professor Temkin. Mark Walker's eyes followed the others and focused on Professor Temkin.

"I've got documentation of conspiracy dating back years. It's enough to cause one hell of a shit storm. I'll fill you in on the details when you get out of here."

"When does it look like I'll get out of here?" asked Professor Walker.

"The doctor said it will probably be a couple of days before they release you," answered Malcolm.

A nurse poked her head into the room. "Visiting hours are over." They said their goodbyes and walked out into the hall.

"How about a drink Professor?" Malcolm asked Professor Temkin.

"I think I'm going to get some rest. As crazy as it's been, it's going to get crazier. I'm not as young as you two."

"Sounds like a plan. Meet for breakfast?"

"Sure. That sounds good."

Out in the hospital parking lot, Stephanie and Malcolm said their goodbyes to Professor Temkin as he got in his car and pulled away. Malcolm and Stephanie also left the hospital, heading in the opposite direction towards their hotel and towards a place to get a nightcap before calling it a night.

A couple of minutes into his drive, Professor Temkin noticed a police cruiser following him. He looked down and kept his speed 2 miles per hour below the speed limit. Moments later, the lights on the patrol car began to flash. He pulled over to the side, put his hands on the steering wheel and waited. Sixty seconds after he stopped, two policemen approached the car. Their guns weren't drawn but each clearly had a hand on their weapon.

"Is there a problem officer?" Professor Temkin asked.

"Please step out of the car," said the policeman who approached him. The other was near the rear of Professor Temkin's car on the opposite side.

"What is the problem officer?" Professor Temkin asked. The officer then drew his weapon.

"Get out of the car!" the officer repeated with harshness in his tone.

The professor slowly opened his car door and put up his hands. "There must be a mistake. What is the problem officer?" The officer grabbed the professor and made him face the side of his car.

"Put your hands on the car. Spread your legs! Don't move." The officer then began to frisk him. When finished, he grabbed Professor Temkin's left wrist, put it behind his back, placed the handcuffs on and then repeated the same action with Professor Temkin's right arm.

"Am I under arrest?" Professor Temkin asked.

"You are not under arrest. This is for our safety," the officer said. He then escorted him back to the police car and put him in the back of their sedan.

A few minutes later the officer that had been taking a back-up position called the other to him. Professor Temkin watched as one officer placed several items on the professor's trunk. They both glanced back at the professor. The officer that had placed him in the back of the police cruiser approached and opened the back door.

"Come with me," he said. When they got to the rear of Professor Temkin's vehicle, he asked, "Can you explain this?" Professor Temkin looked down at the trunk of his car and saw a handgun and a clear plastic package with white powder.

"This isn't mine," said Professor Temkin. The other officer sliced into the side of the package. With a dropper, he put a couple of drops of a liquid onto the powder. Where the liquid touched, it turned blue. "This is about 2 pounds of cocaine," the officer said. The officer standing by Professor Temkin read him the Miranda Rights and put him back in the police car. Professor Temkin knew that he had been framed. He also knew that protesting at this point would do him no good.

Chapter 47

Two days after being notified of her ex-husband's suicide, Synthia received a letter in the mail. There was no return address on it, but she recognized the handwriting. It was Bruce. With shaking hands, Synthia opened the envelope.

My dearest Synthia,

By the time you read this, you will have gotten the news of my death. My dear, I have always loved you deeper than life itself. This time apart has continued to torment me. I think daily about the first night we met. I had not, nor have I since, ever beheld someone more beautiful. I was attracted to you immediately, but throughout that first night, my admiration deepened as I learned about the woman behind that beautiful face. This admiration and love only deepened beyond what I ever thought possible during the years we spent together. Synthia, you are a strong, loving woman, who has given her all for our family. Believe in yourself. Know what I know. Follow your dreams, and above all, be happy. We have made two beautiful children. Tyson and Rex hold a sacred spot deep within my heart. There are no two young men that I would ever think more highly of and feel more deeply for. I allowed myself to get caught up in a situation that has had the potential to hurt a lot of people. I have finally gained the courage to make the choice that I've known I needed to make. As much as I hate to put you and our boys through this, I see no other way to protect my family than what I have done in taking my own life. The people I've worked for are dangerous. There is nothing they wouldn't do to ensure total submission to their cause. I am sorry for the pain I put you through that led up to our separation. But, you must know that I left to protect you and our boys from the people that control our water ways. Included with this letter, you will find information on a life insurance policy I took out in the weeks before I left our home. There should be enough to help ease the burden you are left with in raising our children. Until we meet again, my love will continue for you into the next realm.

Undeniably yours,
Bruce

Synthia read those final words through streaming tears and heart-wrenching sobs. That evening she spoke with her children about their father and the love and admiration he still has for each of them. "Your father is a hero. Always remember that. Always remember how much he has always loved and believed in both of you."

That night they cried and slept snuggling together in Synthia's bed.

Chapter 48

After grabbing a drink, both Stephanie and Malcolm walked into the lobby of their hotel when Malcolm's phone rang.

"Hello, this is Malcolm."

"Malcolm, I've been framed for possession of an illegal firearm and felony possession of cocaine. They also asked me about papers." A voice burst in from the background.

"Why is he on the phone? Get him the fuck off the phone."

Professor Temkin continued in a hushed and hurried tone. "Remember the night we met and the story I told you…about why I left my family?"

"Yes," Malcolm answered.

"Remember that Malcolm. It will lead you…" Silence followed that last word as the call went dead.

"What's wrong?" asked Stephanie. Malcolm told her about Professor Temkin's arrest. "We need to go down to the police station," said Stephanie.

They both started back towards their car.

"Wait," said Malcolm. "We can't go down there. If they did this to Professor Temkin and Professor Walker, they can do it to us." They sat silent and frozen for a moment, not sure what to do.

"They know, Stephanie. They knew about the papers."

"How? How could they know that?" she asked.

"The hospital. It had to be the hospital."

"But nobody was in Professor Walker's room when we spoke to him, and we didn't say anything worth anything outside of that hospital room," Stephanie said. Again, they stood silent, thinking.

"It must have been bugged." Stephanie nodded her head in agreement. "Let's get our stuff from the room and get out of here."

Stephanie and Malcolm continued down the hotel lobby and pushed the elevator button to go up toward the third floor where they were staying. On the way up, Malcolm asked,

"At the hospital, did we mention where we were staying?"

"I don't remember," Stephanie answered.

"Think."

"Yes," she said. "I said if you need anything, we'll be at the La Quinta on Grant… shit."

The elevator door opened and they stepped out onto the third floor. They cautiously walked down the hall towards their room. As they looked around the corner, into the corridor of their room, they saw room 327, the room they were staying in. The door to the room was slightly open. It was only 15 feet from where they both stood. The elevator was at least another 60 feet away. Both Malcolm and Stephanie looked around for a quick way out. In order to get to the exit stairs, they would have to walk across the hall in full view from their room. They jogged towards the elevator. Just as they started down the corridor, they heard men's voices talking and coming their way. The nook for the ice and vending machines was on their left. Stephanie slid in, grabbed Malcolm's hand and pulled him in with her.

There was a two-foot-deep and one and a half foot wide space between the hallway wall and the ice machine. They slid in, Stephanie first, Malcolm next. It barely hid their bodies from a side view. If the men walked past and looked back, Malcolm would be in plain view. They heard the men continue to approach. Both Malcolm and Stephanie scarcely breathed. They both watched the back of the two men as they walked toward the elevator. It was Agent Watson and Agent Sikes. The two men got in the elevator and the door began to close. Just as the door was about to shut, Agent Sikes yelled out, "Hey!" But they were too late. The elevator door closed. Malcolm and Stephanie ran to the exit stairs and started down. Stephanie stopped Malcolm at the second floor. "They will be looking for us in the lobby and on the third floor," she said.

They ran down the halls on the second floor to the exit stairs, directly opposite of the elevator and south of the stairs they had just come down. They scrambled to the bottom and out the exit door at the ground level in back of the hotel and ran. While running down the street, Malcolm spotted a taxi. He flagged it down. Once inside, they both breathed a small sigh of relief. "Where to?" asked the taxi driver. "What motels are nearby?" Malcolm asked. The taxi driver offered a few suggestions, and they settled on a nearby Motel 6.

After being dropped off at the Motel 6, the relief that Malcolm and Stephanie had begun to feel, settled in further.

"Holy shit that was crazy. What do we do now?" asked Stephanie.

"Let's get to our room and figure that out inside."

Once in their room, Malcolm sat in a chair between the bed and the motel window. Stephanie sat back on the bed. Malcolm started by saying,

"Professor Temkin told me to remember the first time we met and what he told me happened to his son. He said that will lead us to what's been going on."

"What happened?" Stephanie asked.

"His son was killed and a cross was set to fire on his front lawn."

"Wow," Stephanie said with a look of shock on her face.

"Wow is right. But what is it about that that we need to know?"

"What was his son's name?" Stephanie asked.

"Abraham Temkin."

"Could it be related to something about him? Maybe a memorial or something?"

"I don't know," said Malcolm, "There was Abraham, a burning cross, and there were scriptures carved into the porch where Abraham lay dead."

"What were the scriptures?"

"It was from the 10 commandments, if I remember right," Malcolm said. "I need a Bible." Stephanie leaned over to the bedside drawers and pulled the top drawer open. Inside, there was a Bible left by the Gideons. "Thank God for the Gideons," she said.

Malcolm stood up and took the Bible from Stephanie. He flipped through the pages to Deuteronomy.

"Here they are. It was a scolding and a warning for publishing his findings about the problems with the flu vaccine they were working on. Deuteronomy 5:20 *"Thou shalt not bear false witness against thy neighbor"* and 5:7 *"Thou shalt have no other gods before me."*

"Do you have any idea what they could mean?" Stephanie asked.

"No idea," Malcolm answered. "Let's take tonight to think about it. We can also see if we can find any other clues in Professor Temkin's hotel room early in the morning."

Both Malcolm and Stephanie got ready for bed using the complimentary toothbrush and toothpaste they had gotten from the front desk. After brushing their teeth, they each got in bed and held each other. Stephanie started crying, "Are we going to be alright Malcolm?"

"Everything is going to be okay," Malcolm answered. "Trust me," and he squeezed her tight. After several minutes of silence, Stephanie asked,

"How are we going to get to Professor Temkin's apartment without a car?"

Malcolm thought for a moment, "I've got an idea for that. But, for now, let's get some rest." With Stephanie's head on his chest, Malcolm played with her hair in an attempt to comfort her. He still struggled with what had happened between them, but he also knew how much emotional weight she carried with all that was going on. After a while, he heard the deep breathing of sleep coming from Stephanie. Malcolm closed his eyes and soon sleep found him as well.

The next morning, they took a taxi to Malcolm's apartment building. He didn't plan on going inside and just directed the taxi to stop in front of an old faded gold Toyota Corolla. It was Cliff's car. Malcolm got out of the car, knelt down and reached for something up under the rear bumper. "Bingo," he said. Stephanie could see the spare key to the Corolla in his hand as he held it up. Stephanie and Malcolm each got in. Inside, the black seats were withered and ripped and the dash was cracked. Malcolm put the key in and turned the ignition. It cranked weakly but didn't start. He tried again, pumping the gas. This time it fired up. Malcolm and Stephanie each let out a sigh of relief. Malcolm put the car in gear, backed up and then started the drive toward the hotel that Professor Temkin had been staying in. As they slowly drove by, Stephanie saw a problem.

"They're here."

"What?" Malcolm asked.

"Keep driving. They're here." She pointed at the black sedan that was identical to the one Agents Sikes and Watson drove. It was very out of place, parked in this low budget motel building.

"Well, where to now?" Malcolm asked. "Let's go to the library," Stephanie answered. They drove on and continued to the Denver University library with plans to try to decipher Professor Temkin's code. Once inside the library they each searched every combination of *cross, fire, Denver, Abraham, Deuteronomy 5:7, Deuteronomy 5:20,* and *10 Commandments* on the web. The only plausible things they found were an Abraham Synagogue in Denver and a Ten Commandments Monument outside of the Colorado State Capitol building. They decided to check out the synagogue first.

Thirty minutes after leaving the library, they pulled up outside of a red brick building. The star of David was prominent in the center of the building directly over the entryway, which was highlighted by a white column on each side. Above the front entryway were several words in Hebrew. "Well, let's hope we're right," said Malcolm. Malcolm parked the Corolla and they both stepped out of the vehicle and walked towards the entrance. Once at the entrance of the synagogue, they were approached by a man wearing a black suit. He had a long grey beard and wore a yarmulke on his head. They assumed he was the Rabbi.

"Welcome," the man said.

"Thank you. A friend of ours may have visited or sent something here that he asked us to retrieve," said Malcolm.

"What is your friend's name?" asked the Rabbi.

"Edward Temkin." The Rabbi sat silent for a bit.

"When would your friend have visited?" he asked.

"It would have been within the last couple of days. Again, the Rabbi paused to think.

"I'm sorry, I can't help you. There has not been anyone introducing themselves to me by that name, and I definitely have not received anything to hold for anyone." Stephanie and Malcolm stood there a moment longer, racking their mind as to anything else they should say or ask.

Stephanie spoke, "Thank you for your time." Malcolm and Stephanie both walked away from the synagogue a little deflated, but still optimistic that the 10 Commandments Memorial may provide some direction. Once back inside the car, they searched the address for the State Capitol building on their mobile phones and drove to the location.

Malcolm and Stephanie arrived at the State Capitol building a little before 11:00 AM. The Capitol building was a large white granite structure with a dome roof in the center. A stone staircase lead up from the grounds to the entrance. Trees highlighted the entrance on each side. Parks also surrounded the

Capitol grounds. Adjacent to the Capitol, and technically still part of the State Capitol grounds was Lincoln Park, where the 10 Commandments Memorial was said to be located. As they looked upon the grounds, there were people walking in and out of the building. Within the adjoining grass areas, there were people touring the grounds, running, walking dogs, painting on canvas, and a group throwing a frisbee to each other.

Stephanie and Malcolm got out of the car and walked past the Capitol building and across the immediate grounds. They reached Lincoln Street on the west side, near where the park was located. They crossed Lincoln Street and entered Lincoln Park. After a bit of looking around, they found the monument they were looking for. Given its location, not far off from two intersecting paths, many people walked past and around that monument.

An elderly woman, wearing a pink shawl, white blouse, and a pink skirt gently approached everyone who stopped near the 10 Commandments Monument. "Who was it who died on the cross?" she would ask. Many people ignored her, but some answered "Jesus," to which she would reply "God bless," and handed out a card that had a picture of Jesus on the cross. Malcolm and Stephanie moved closer and studied everything on and around the monument. Besides the stone monument, with the 10 Commandments scribed upon it, they could not see anything that could give them more direction. The elderly woman engaged them. "Who was it who died on the cross?" she asked. Malcolm said "Jesus?" "God bless," she replied, and proceeded to hand him the card with Jesus on the cross.

Now right next to the monument, Malcolm and Stephanie both continued to study it. Still nothing of significance came to either one of them.

"You find any clues?" Malcolm asked Stephanie.

"No," she answered and they began to walk away.

"Wait," said Stephanie as she turned around and faced the elderly woman near the monument. The elderly woman looked into Stephanie's eyes and asked,

"Who was it who died on the cross?"

"Abraham," Stephanie answered.

"Abraham who?" the old woman asked.

"Abraham Temkin," Stephanie answered.

The old woman smiled and said, "Come with me."

Chapter 49

Stephanie and Malcolm followed the woman toward another part of the Capitol grounds. Stephanie noticed a bag with the strap draped across the old woman's left shoulder with the compartment of the bag resting on her right hip. She had handed out the cards from this bag. Stephanie now wondered if there was more to it. They stopped at a park bench and the old woman sat.

"Please sit," she said. Both Malcolm and Stephanie sat on the bench next to her. "It appears we have a mutual friend," said the old woman. She didn't make eye contact and kept her gaze forward. Malcolm and Stephanie continued to look at her awaiting what would happen next. "Please look forward and relax," the old woman said. She took out a plastic bag that had the crust-ends from several loaves of bread. As she started tossing small pieces of bread-crust that she'd ripped off, pigeons gathered around.

"Edward Temkin is a very long-time friend of mine. He told me that if I did not hear from him every morning at 7:00 am, I should look for a young couple, like yourselves, that would come with his son's name at the 10 Commandment Memorial. It is possible that there are people watching, that's why it's important to act as if we aren't conversing. I am leaving you a key. Don't pick it up in a way that people can tell what you are doing." She sat a small key down on the bench between her and Stephanie. Stephanie crossed her leg and put her hand on the bench, palm down, over the key. She adjusted and held the key in her palm. "The key is to a safe deposit box at Wells Fargo on the corner of Grant and 17th Avenue. Edward said that you would need to let the world know what you find there."

"How do we do that?" asked Stephanie.

"Oh, I'm sure that you'll figure that out." There was a pause in their discussion, while the old woman continued to feed the pigeons. "You should go now. God be with you both."

Malcolm and Stephanie stood up and walked back toward their car. Malcolm got into the driver's seat and Stephanie sat on the passenger side.

"We need to make sure that nobody is following us," Malcolm said. They sat there for several minutes and looked around the capitol grounds.

"I think they know where we are," said Stephanie. "Look." Walking through the grounds were two men in suits. They were not Agents Watson and Sikes, but they looked like they were from the same mold.

"But how could they know?" asked Malcolm. At that moment a text rang on Malcolm's phone. It was Reggie asking how Malcolm was holding up. Stephanie immediately looked at her phone and then proceeded to turn it off. She then looked at Malcolm and said, "Turn your phone off. They're probably tracking our phones." Malcolm held the power button down and shut the phone down. They both watched the men. They looked as if they were talking to someone from their headsets.

"That's exactly what they were doing," said Malcolm. He started up the car and drove away from the Capitol building. After driving a few miles, he pulled over and stopped at a park just to watch the vehicles around him pass and to see if anybody appeared to be following them. When 15 minutes had passed, they were satisfied and started their way to Wells Fargo on Grant and 17th Avenue. As they approached, the bank looked like one of the original Wells Fargo's in Colorado. The building was old, but it had distinct architecture and design within the concrete and brick walls that made it unique. Malcolm parked and Stephanie opened her door.

"Are you coming Malcolm?"

"No, I better stay. If a black man comes in with some safe deposit box key, they'll think I stole it from someone." He smiled.

"Come on," Stephanie said.

"I'm not kidding," replied Malcolm, "I'm staying here." Stephanie walked into the bank alone. Several minutes later, she came out with an accordion style folder filled with documents.

Once she was back inside the car, they drove towards their motel. As they approached the turn-in to the motel parking lot, Malcolm slowed down and came to a stop. A car honked behind him and then drove around their vehicle. Both Stephanie and Malcolm saw it. In the parking lot was an out of place black town car. The man in the front seat of that black sedan picked up his phone and within seconds Agent Sikes came running out from Malcolm and Stephanie's motel room. Malcolm hit the gas and turned right down the first street he came to. He made three more rights, making a full circle around the block, which put them right back at the Motel 6. The agents were gone.

"What are you doing?" asked Stephanie.

"This is the last place they would think we would go."

"Yeah, it's the last place I would go after seeing them in our room."

Malcolm parked the car in the back of the motel, out of sight from anyone looking from the road or even from the side of their motel room.

"Stay here. I'm going to get our things," said Malcolm.

"What if they come back?"

"Then I'll hide under the bed," he said as he winked at her.

Within 30 seconds of Malcolm going inside their motel room, Agents Watson and Sikes pulled up. They sat in their car and seemed to be watching the road, probably waiting to see if Malcolm and Stephanie came back. Stephanie watched in panic, hoping that Malcolm would notice their car before coming out.

That didn't happen. When Malcolm walked out of the motel room, both Agents drew their sidearms, directing Malcolm to his knees then onto his belly with arms and legs spread. While they dealt with Malcolm and were in the process of putting him in their car, Stephanie started up the Corolla and exited the opposite side of the motel, where they would not be able to see her leave.

Stephanie knew that the only real possibility of saving her friends and in ending this mess would be to expose what was going on in every way possible. She drove to the University of Denver library and spent the next few hours reading and scanning the most damning documents that Professor Temkin had marked within the stolen documents. From there she uploaded the documents online and sent copies of it to every news organization she could find, focusing on those that had continued to focus on real news, specifically CNS, which she suspected had the followership of those not impacted by the chemicals so many had been exposed to. Stephanie then published links to the documents on multiple social media outlets, including Twitter.

She continued to scan and send the documents into as many hands as possible, staying at the DU library until it closed. At that point, now exhausted, she took the documents she held in her hand, along with an extra hard copy, and found another Motel 6 on the other side of town.

Inside her motel room, Stephanie again felt the weight of the entire situation upon her. She cried, and for the first time in years, she prayed. She prayed for Malcolm, Professor Walker,

Professor Temkin, her father, her sister, her nephew, and all the people impacted by what had been going on with this numbing of society. When she finished praying, she reflected even more deeply. What the government has been doing artificially for decades, so many individuals choose to do on their own. She had done it. She had lived it...lost in doing, lost in thinking, and avoiding all that is part of the here and now. Stephanie felt the warmth of deep connectedness that she only remembered feeling a few other times before now. She felt it on the morning walks with her father in the hills near her house. She felt it while watching the hummingbirds feed at her childhood home, and while sitting out on that rock, waiting for the taxi to pick her up from a night her body still felt sore from.

Stephanie didn't feel guilty anymore. Acceptance is something that she heard of, but never contemplated like she did at this moment. She saw it as the one way to place herself in a position to change life for the better...to control her fate. There are still good things in this world. Rajan had helped her recognize that through his positive outlook in the most dire situations. There are things about now, with the world and with herself that she did not like. But accepting and acknowledging where she is right now and right here, she could begin to move forward, even though she was not sure what that next step would bring. What she did know and feel, is that it would be a move forward...and that is what she longed for.

At this moment Stephanie understood at a level that seemed to transcend her own mind. She, and others, were part of something, and this something connected them all. She thought back to so many times that she had judged others. Sometimes vocally, other times, just in her head. She judged others that had done much less of what society deemed as wrong than she had done over the previous two weeks. As a child, her father had read her *To Kill a Mockingbird* on several occasions. The words from Atticus Finch now resonated so much more than it ever had. *"You never really understand a person until you consider things from his point of view--until you climb inside of his skin and walk around in it."* She had "climbed inside and walked around in it." If nothing else, she had perspective she had never had…and for that, she was thankful.

Stephanie hoped that she and Malcolm could work things out and that he could get past what had happened between them. But, somehow, she knew, even if he never really accepted her again, she would be okay. Life could be okay. With this in her mind, Stephanie closed her eyes and fell soundly asleep…this despite all that was going on around her.

When Stephanie woke up, she turned on the news. The story she had worked so hard to get out was being covered. She drove back to the Wells Fargo they had visited the day before and put the original copy back in the safe deposit box. After leaving the bank, she turned her phone back on. Online, the news had spread like wildfire with the CDC, EPA, and Executive Branch of the United States government all under fire from the press.

By the afternoon, Stephanie had an interview on CNS, where she discussed the basics of what had happened over the weeks leading up to this point and pled for the release of Malcolm Wright, Mark Walker, and Edward Temkin. By the following morning, all were released. When Stephanie picked them up from the police station, they were a little bruised, battered and tired, but exuberant to see the unraveling of what they had worked so hard to put a stop to. After getting cleaned up and gathering a fresh pair of clothes, all four gathered at Mark Walker's house to watch as members of congress, as well as the President of the United States, profess in front of the world, their deep regret for this terrible conspiracy. They expressed their commitment to detain all involved and to put protective measures in place to ensure nothing like this could happen again.

They all listened to promises that each one of our country's leaders professed, but Mark, Edward, Stephanie, and Malcolm all had difficulty believing, and in fact, they suspected many of those expressing vocal outrage were likely involved, at least in some way. But, in another sense, Stephanie thought to herself, when it came to the lulling that occurred within society, both artificial as well as self-induced, who wasn't?

Chapter 50

The next day Malcolm went to visit Cliff at the Denver County Jail. After checking in and being searched, he was escorted to the visitation area where the officer sat him down at a table. A few minutes later, Cliff came into the room.

"Hey what's happenin Maw? I hear you're famous now?"

"How you holdin up brotha?"

"Three square meals a day," Cliff said while attempting a smile, but Malcolm could see the heartache through it.

"I spoke to Coach Rand before heading in. He said he's been working with Coach Sloan and has been able to generate a lot more support for you with all that's come out these last couple of days."

"Coach Rand is a good man."

Malcolm then spoke quietly, but seriously, "You saved me, Cliff. I never thanked you for that. Thank you."

"Ah, it ain't nothin."

"No, it's a lot, and you're in here because of it."

Both sat quietly for a minute not really sure what to say.

"Cliff, it's not likely that you'll finish football at DU, but you gotta go pro man. The talent you've got is just somethin."

"I think it's the end of my playin career Maw. Ain't nobody wanna felon on the team."

"You watch the news? You know that's not true!" Malcolm said, and they both laughed. Then it turned serious again.

"Those felons ain't never got caught for killin no one."

"Even if you weren't 6'7", I'd still look up to you, Cliff. You've got talent like I've never seen. But, that all aside, with what you've done…from where you've come from…is something people just don't do. You're something special, Cliff. Never forget that." Tears started welling up in Cliff's eyes. Malcolm had never seen this man cry before.

"Between Coach Rand and us bringing light to what happened, we're gonna get you outta here. You start planning what you're gonna do. You're gonna have a chance to do something big. You just have to do it. Do it for all those who stay stuck in the projects and never get a chance." Cliff nodded his head, "Thanks brotha."

Thirty days after Malcolm visited Cliff in jail, he was out. Though expelled from DU for illegal possession of a firearm, he still cheered on his team from the sidelines for the rest of the season. The following spring, Cliff signed with the Cleveland Browns, where he not only played, but continued to dominate the line for 8 years in the pros. During his career, he spent some of the off-season running football camps and helping high school players in the rough neighborhoods near where he grew up, but he spent just as much time with those that did not have the physical talent to become stars on the field. He was quoted as saying, *"Some are blessed with ability that can be highlighted on the field, some are blessed with the ability to solve problems and create solutions for the world to use, and ALL are blessed by being part of what unites us all...that part of us, that makes each one of us INCREDIBLE. Always remember that. Know that. Feel that. Embrace that. And, BE that. You are important because of who you are, beyond the abilities and limitations your body and your mind provides you."*

Cliff spoke to many schools in the area to give hope to those who had none. "If I can just help one kid, who's been beat down and told that he's no good, realize he's incredible, I'll die a happy man," Cliff had said when being interviewed about his community involvement. By the end of his pro-career, he had inspired many to reach for more and to realize their worth, whether on the football field, in the classroom, or within the community.

After Cliff's football career, he worked with Coach Rand for several years helping to coach football at his old high school. When Coach Rand retired, Cliff accepted the head football coaching position and taught physical education, having finished his degree, while working as an assistant coach. At age 48, Cliff died of a sudden heart attack, which has unfortunately been a trend with NFL linemen post retirement. Cliff's memorial took place at

FirstEnergy Stadium, where the Cleveland Browns play. Every seat in the place was taken, as a testament of the *Incredible* that Cliff had helped so many realize within themselves.

Chapter 51

In the weeks following the initial press releases, and after the constant outrage and mock-outrage, spewed from those trying to maintain or obtain a voice and power with the people, life seemed to be going back to "normal" for the rest of the world. But, for Malcolm, nothing would be the same again. He learned more about people, psychology, sociology and himself over this last month, than he had learned throughout his high school and college career combined. But, there were things he had let sit that he couldn't let sit any longer. There were things that he wanted to do and be that he couldn't do and be until he confronted that which sat in the back recesses of his mind.

Malcolm got in his car and drove. He drove throughout the night. Early the next morning, he found himself sitting in his car on a street bordering a park. Across the street was Harold's house. Harold lived in a town just outside of Ogden, UT. Malcolm had known where he had moved to, but never confronted the man who had abused him as a child. "It was the past and already done," he had told himself. Harold was just a teen when he had committed these acts.

There Malcolm sat without a plan and without any idea of what he would do. He just knew he had to do something. He felt it deep inside and wouldn't ignore it this time. After sitting for an hour or so, Malcolm saw Harold leave his house in his truck, most likely going to work, where he did various types of construction. About an hour or two after Harold left, their garage door opened and two young girls, who looked to be around 8 and 10 years old, came riding out on bikes to go to school. The girls' mother, Harold's wife, Olivia, followed, waving goodbye to her girls.

After the girls got a block or two away from their home, Malcolm got out of his car and approached Olivia.

"Hello Olivia, I'm Malcolm. Harold is my father's brother."

"Yes, hi Malcolm. What brings you here? It's been a long time since I've seen you. You're all grown up."

Malcolm smiled and said, "Can we talk?" Olivia invited Malcolm into her home, and over the next few hours, Malcolm shared some of the abuse that he had experienced as a young boy with Harold.

"Olivia, I hate to bring this up to you, but something has been telling me deep inside myself that I need to…and it goes beyond me."

Olivia began to cry and the crying turned to sobbing. Malcolm touched Olivia's shoulder and said, "he hasn't stopped, has he?"

"I don't think so. I don't know for sure, but I've been wondering."

"You owe it to your girls to find out."

"I know," she said through her sobs.

While Malcolm waited outside their home, Olivia went to her daughters' elementary school and had a counselor call them into the office. There, with the help of the counselor, the secrets were revealed. Harold would not be allowed to harm her daughters again. That afternoon, Harold and Olivia's daughters were dropped off at a friend's house. At Harold's house Malcolm, Olivia, and two police officers stayed waiting in the front room when Harold arrived home from work.

Harold rushed into the house. "Is everything alright? What are the police doing here?" Right after saying that, his eyes locked on Malcolm. Malcolm stood.

"Harold, I was young, but I remember everything. It wasn't okay and it impacted my life, but I can accept what has already happened to me." Malcolm paused for a moment and everyone was silent. "What I won't accept is continuing to sit by while you hurt other children, including your own." Harold's eyes were wide and in shock.

"How could you?" Olivia cried. "Our own daughters! How could you?" Harold didn't deny it. He just hung his head and stood silent. The two police officers handcuffed, arrested Harold and escorted him into their squad car. Malcolm and Olivia stood on the front porch as they drove away.

Chapter 52

As Malcolm finished packing up his apartment, all that was left was a shelf full of books. As he grabbed an armload off of one side, the half empty shelf tipped up on the empty side and spilled the rest of the books on the floor. Malcolm put the books he held in his arms in a box and then began picking up the fallen books from the floor. While picking up and placing the books into the box, he noticed one sprawled open. It was *The Book of Mormon*. Highlighted in yellow, he saw the words, "And others will he pacify, and lull them away into carnal security that they will say: All is well in Zion; yea, Zion prospereth, all is well—and thus the devil cheateth their souls, and leadeth them away carefully down to hell" 2 Nephi 28:21. He stopped and pondered those words, his experiences over this last month, and in years past with organized religion. He smiled to himself and closed the book on that chapter.

He put the shelf back on the wall and placed *The Book of Mormon* there. The shelf was now empty, except for that book. He had moved on. He was no longer living within that false reality. No longer was he gripped within the confirmation bias and obedience, based on fear and shame that he had allowed "leaders" to entice him to submit to. It was not their fault. He felt no more resentment in his heart. In fact, he felt sorry for them. All of them were still caught within their own head and false world, not really living. At the same time, Malcolm knew that their true self was still within every one of them, waiting to be freed.

Malcolm taped up the box and looked around the room. There was one more book halfway under the bed. He grabbed it. *The Book of Awakening* by Mark Nepo. He opened its pages and read one more highlighted quote. "'Enlightenment for a wave is the moment the wave realizes that it is water. At that moment all fear of death disappears'-- Thich Nhat Hanh." He placed it on top of the box and picked the box up. As he left his apartment, he didn't even look back inside. He set the box down, closed and locked the door and took a moment to take in all that was around him. Malcolm consciously took in deep breaths and felt life flow through him.

"Are you ready?" he heard a voice calling from down the stairs. It was Stephanie. "I'm on my way!" He took in one more deep breath and walked down the stairs. When he reached the moving truck, Stephanie was already in the passenger seat. Malcolm put the box in the back, closed and latched the door, and hopped into the driver's seat. "I love you, honey," said Stephanie as she grabbed his hand and leaned over to kiss him. "I love you more." Malcolm started the truck and they started toward their new home.

Epilogue

Even before completing his bachelor's degree, Malcolm began writing. He integrated real-life psychological, emotional, and sociological numbing that takes place naturally and integrated those into gripping fictional novels. It proved to be a release for Malcolm, but it also worked to raise awareness and add to the movement of embracing and accepting the present moment. His first publication came one year after completing his Bachelor's Degree. The publicity he had received after the documents were released to the press, helped him solidify publication and a quick following. While writing, Malcolm continued his studies, finishing his Master's Degree in Sociology two years after his Bachelors' Degree. He continued his study and later obtained his Ph.D. In addition to writing, Malcolm began to teach Sociology courses at the University of Colorado in Boulder.

Upon finishing her Bachelor's Degree that year, Stephanie immediately began working with Mark Walker. She started out assisting with women and couples dealing with the loss of their child, but soon created another arm of their work to include women and female teens who had suffered abuse, sexual, physical, and psychological. This quickly grew from a couple of working groups twice a month to her full time passion. Stephanie recruited and trained others to complement the movement aimed at helping these women move past their abusive history and to realize their worth, their talents, and to proactively follow their passions.

Immediately following graduation, Malcolm and Stephanie had married. Stephanie's father had passed away within a few months past the apathy documents becoming public. With her father gone, Professor Walker walked Stephanie down the aisle at her wedding. Cliff served as Malcolm's best man. With a reestablished relationship, absent the effects of the emotional numbing, Kathy Petersen was Stephanie's maid of honor.

Now that all of the requirements were in place, with a stable home and stable income, first with Stephanie's career and later with Malcolm's writings, they were able to become foster parents for Jamin and Ryan. One year after graduating with their bachelors, both children were successfully adopted and became a permanent part of their family.

Professor Temkin reestablished a relationship with his daughter and a friendship with his former wife. They would not remarry. The scars and memories were too deep for Maria, but they spoke often, even traveling together with their daughter in the years that followed. Not long after the release of the government documents, Professor Temkin's credibility was reestablished.

Soon after, he accepted an endowed chair position at the University of California Berkeley, where he reestablished his work within medical research.

Thank you for reading. Please share your thoughts, feelings, and opinions with me at CYFworld.com

Continue reading for some of the inspirational quotes and ideas for life found throughout this novel.

Know – Accept – Apply - Thrive

"Some are blessed with ability that can be highlighted on the field, some are blessed with the ability to solve problems and create solutions for the world to use, and ALL are blessed by being part of what unites us all…that part of us, that makes each one of us INCREDIBLE. Always remember that. Know that. Feel that. Embrace that. And, BE that. You are important because of who you are, beyond the abilities and limitations your body and your mind provide you." – Cliff Patterson

"Believe in yourself. Know what I know. Follow your dreams, and above all, be happy" – Bruce Dobson

"It doesn't matter what happens, you CAN STILL WIN!" - Rajan

"Every time the sun comes up, look for something you didn't see before. If you look to see something new, something beautiful, you

will always find it." – Mike Petersen

"There are times, sometimes very long times, that we forget who we are, where we come from, and what we are a part of. Sometimes we feel dead in a sense, but there is always a rebirth, a remembering from that part of us that never forgets." – Mike Petersen

"You don't need anyone else to obtain all that God is or has. It's within you. It's a part of you." - Mike Petersen

"At this moment, you are where you are meant to be ...when you realize that, life happens." – Eckhart Tolle

"Follow your Bliss and the Universe will open doors where there were only walls." – Joseph Campbell

"If I were not afraid, if I were not alone, what would I do at this moment?" – unknown

"Enlightenment for a wave is the moment wave realizes that it is water. At that moment all fear of death disappears." –Thich Nhat Hanh.

"The mind and the body are linked. Use your body to expel all

that anger, hurt and pain your mind has refused to let go. It's not about forgetting, it's about moving forward...taking control of your future." - Mark Walker

"You never really understand a person until you consider things from his point of view--until you climb inside of his skin and walk around in it." - To Kill a Mockingbird

"While judgment continues to be held due to the physical or psychological characteristics of a person, without the true realization of the deep connection that we all share, the enlightened and inner peaceful state that one may desire will continue to elude the person seeking it." – Malcolm Wright

CYFworld

Join the CYFworld community at https://CYFworld.com

Vision and Purpose

We CAN all control our reality and obtain true personal fulfillment, regardless of the circumstances that we have been placed within. We will not blindly follow the plan that others have for us, nor will we embrace words of discouragement that keeps us from fulfilling our own *Personal Legend, "and when we let our own light shine, we unconsciously give other people permission to do the same" (Marianne Williamson).* We will unite with others with a similar mission and organize a community that will change the world for the positive, one small act at a time.

ABOUT THE AUTHOR

Travis Jensen is an innovator with a passion for real and positive change. Life experiences offered perspective early on, where even in his childhood journal he wrote, "it's as if I was put here on earth to help others." He developed CYFworld as a concept to create space and unity among those with a desire to embrace who we truly are and the connection we all share. With this concept, he works with others to offer resources that enable individuals to determine their own reality, regardless of their current place in life. Travis has lead teams of individuals in creating positive change. With his father an outdoorsman and his mother a teacher and author, he gained a passion for both, where he finds his release through writing and spending time in the mountains of Northern Arizona. Today, he lives in Phoenix with 8 children, as part of a blended family, and his life's partner and soulmate.

www.ingramcontent.com/pod-product-compliance
Lightning Source LLC
Chambersburg PA
CBHW071119170626
46809CB00002B/431